"Romance, vi... really who could ask for more?"
—Debbie Macomber, #1 *New York Times* bestselling author, on *Blackberry Summer*

"This quirky, funny, warmhearted romance will draw readers in and keep them enthralled to the last romantic page."
—*Library Journal* on *Christmas in Snowflake Canyon*

"Entertaining, heart-wrenching, and totally involving, [*Evergreen Springs*] is a sure winner."
—*Library Journal*

"A sometimes heartbreaking tale of love and relationships in a small Colorado town.... Poignant and sweet."
—*Publishers Weekly* on *Christmas in Snowflake Canyon*

"RaeAnne Thayne is quickly becoming one of my favorite authors... Once you start reading, you aren't going to be able to stop."
—*Fresh Fiction* on *Snow Angel Cove*

"Plenty of tenderness and Colorado sunshine flavor this pleasant escape."
—*Publishers Weekly* on *Woodrose Mountain*

"Thayne, once again, delivers a heartfelt story of a caring community and a caring romance between adults who have triumphed over tragedies."
—*Booklist* on *Woodrose Mountain*

"Thayne pens another winner... Her main characters are strong and three-dimensional, with enough heat between them to burn the pages."
—*RT Book Reviews* on *Currant Creek Valley*

Dear Reader,

I'm so excited to bring you the story of Faith Nichols Dustin and Chase Brannon, at long last. I introduced them two years ago in *The Christmas Ranch*, the first book in my current Cold Creek miniseries. I loved Chase and Faith from the beginning. Faith had just suffered a great tragedy and the world seemed a bleak place. Chase was not only her neighbor but her best friend—caring, loyal and fiercely protective of her.

I knew a few basics about their lives and the journey they would have to find happiness again together, but uncovering the details of their story has been a true delight.

I'm always so happy when I have the chance to return to Pine Gulch and visit old friends! It's been ten years since I wrote my first book based in Cold Creek Canyon (I know! I can't believe it, either!) and the people who live here almost feel like family.

Wishing you and your loved ones the very best this holiday season.

*RaeAnne*

# The Holiday Gift

―――

## RaeAnne Thayne

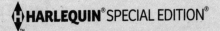

**HARLEQUIN**® SPECIAL EDITION®

Recycling programs
for this product may
not exist in your area.

ISBN-13: 978-0-373-65094-1

The Holiday Gift

Copyright © 2016 by RaeAnne Thayne

Printed in U.S.A.

www.Harlequin.com

**RaeAnne Thayne** finds inspiration in the beautiful northern Utah mountains, where the *New York Times* and *USA TODAY* bestselling author lives with her husband and three children. Her books have won numerous honors, including RITA® Award nominations from Romance Writers of America and a Career Achievement Award from *RT Book Reviews*. RaeAnne loves to hear from readers and can be contacted through her website, raeannethayne.com.

To Lisa Townsend, trainer extraordinaire, who is gorgeous inside and out. And to Jennie, Trudy, Karen, Becky, Jill and everyone else in our group for your example, your encouragement, your friendship, your laughter—and especially for making me look forward to workouts (except the burpees— I'll never look forward to those!).

## Chapter One

Something was wrong, but Faith Dustin didn't have the first idea what.

She glanced at Chase Brannon again, behind the wheel of his pickup truck. Sunglasses shielded his eyes but his strong jaw was still flexed, his shoulders tense.

Since they had left the Idaho Falls livestock auction forty-five minutes earlier, heading back to Cold Creek Canyon, the big rancher hadn't smiled once and had answered most of her questions in monosyllables, his mind clearly a million miles away.

Faith frowned. He wasn't acting at all like himself. They were frequent travel companions, visiting various livestock auctions around the region at least once or twice a month for the last few years. They had even gone on a few buying trips to Denver together, an eight-hour drive from their little corner of eastern Idaho. He was her oldest friend—and had been since she and her sisters came to live with their aunt and uncle nearly two decades ago.

In many ways, she and Chase were really a team and comingled their ranch operations, since his ranch, Brannon Ridge, bordered the Star N on two sides.

Usually when they traveled, they never ran out of things to talk about. Her kids and their current dramas, real or imagined; his daughter, Addie, who lived with her mother in Boise; Faith's sisters and their growing families. Their ranches, the community, the price of beef, their future plans. It was all grist for their conversational mill. She valued his opinion—often she would run ideas past him—and she wanted to think he rated hers as highly.

The drive to Idaho Falls earlier that morning had seemed just like usual, filled with conversation and their usual banter. Everything had seemed normal during the auction. He had stayed right by her side, a quiet, steady support, while she engaged in—and eventually won—a fierce bidding war for a beautiful paint filly with excellent barrel racing bloodlines.

That horse, intended as a Christmas gift for her twelve-year-old daughter, Louisa, was the whole reason they had gone to the auction. Yes, she'd been a little carried away by winning the auction so that she'd hugged him hard and kissed him smack on the lips, but surely that wasn't what was bothering him. She'd kissed and hugged him tons of times.

Okay, maybe she had been careful not to be so casual

with her affection for him the last six or seven months, for reasons she didn't want to explore, but she couldn't imagine he would go all cold and cranky over something as simple as a little kiss.

No. His mood had shifted after that, but all her subtle efforts to wiggle out what was wrong had been for nothing.

His mood certainly matched the afternoon. Faith glanced out at the uniformly gray sky and the few random, hard-edged snowflakes clicking against the windshield. The weather wasn't pleasant but it wasn't horrible either. The snowflakes weren't sticking to the road yet, anyway, though she expected they would see at least a few inches on the ground by morning.

Even the familiar festive streets of Pine Gulch— wreaths hanging on the streetlamps and each downtown business decorated with lights and window dressings— didn't seem to lift his dark mood.

When he hit the edge of town and turned into Cold Creek Canyon toward home, she decided to try one last time to figure out what might be bothering him.

"Did something happen at the auction?"

He glanced away from the road briefly, the expression in his silver-blue eyes shielded by the amber lenses of his sunglasses. "Why would you think that?"

She studied his dearly familiar profile, struck by his full mouth and his tanned, chiseled features—covered now with just a hint of dark afternoon shadow. Funny, how she saw him just about every single day but was sometimes taken by surprise all over again by how great-looking he was.

With his dark, wavy hair covered by the black Stetson he wore, that slow, sexy smile, and his broad shoulders and slim hips, he looked rugged and dangerous and completely male. It was no wonder the waitresses at the café next to the auction house always fought each other to serve their table.

She shifted her attention away from such ridiculous things and back to the conversation. "I don't know. Maybe because that's the longest sentence you've given me since we left Idaho Falls. You've replied to everything else with either a grunt or a monosyllable."

Beneath that afternoon shadow, a muscle clenched in his jaw. "That doesn't mean anything happened. Maybe I'm just not in a chatty mood."

She certainly had days like that. Heaven knew she'd had her share of blue days over the last two and a half years. Through every one of them, Chase had been her rock.

"Nothing wrong with that, I guess. Are you sure that's all? Was it something Beckett McKinley said? I saw him corner you at lunch."

He glanced over at her briefly and again she wished she could see the expression behind his sunglasses. "He wanted to know how I like the new baler I bought this year and he also wanted my opinion on a…personal matter. I told him I liked the baler fine but told him the other thing wasn't any of my damn business."

She blinked at both his clipped tone and the language. Chase didn't swear very often. When he did, there was usually a good reason.

"Now you've got my curiosity going. What kind of

personal matter would Beck want your opinion about? The only thing I can think the man needs is a nanny for those hellion boys of his."

He didn't say anything for a long moment, just watched the road and those snowflakes spitting against windshield. When he finally spoke, his voice was clipped. "It was about you."

She stared. "Me?"

Chase's hands tightened on the steering wheel. "He wants to ask you out, specifically to go as his date to the stockgrowers association's Christmas party on Friday."

If he had just told her Beck wanted her to dress up like a Christmas angel and jump from his barn roof, she wouldn't have been more surprised—and likely would have been far less panicky.

"I... He...what?"

"Beck wants to take you to the Christmas party this weekend. I understand there's going to be dancing and a full dinner this year."

Beck McKinley. The idea of dating the man took her by complete surprise. Yes, he was a great guy, with a prosperous ranch on the other side of Pine Gulch. She considered him a good friend but she had never *once* thought of him in romantic terms.

The unexpected paradigm shift wasn't the only thing bothering her about what Chase had just said.

"Hold on. If he wanted to take me to the party, why wouldn't Beck just ask me himself instead of feeling like he has to go through you first?"

That muscle flexed in his jaw again. "You'll have to ask him that."

The things he wasn't saying in this conversation would fill a radio broadcast. She frowned as Chase pulled into the drive leading to his ranch. "You told him I'm already going with you, didn't you?"

He didn't answer for a long moment. "No," he finally said. "I didn't."

Unease twanged through her, the same vague sense that had haunted her at stray moments for several months. Something was off between her and Chase and, for the life of her, she couldn't put a finger on it.

"Oh. Did you already make plans?" She forced a cheerful smile. "We've gone together the last few years so I just sort of assumed we would go together again this year but I guess we should have talked about it. If you already have something going, don't worry about me. Seriously. I don't mind going by myself. I'll have plenty of other friends there I can sit with. Or I could always skip it and stay home with the kids. Jenna McRaven does a fantastic job with the food and I always enjoy the company of other grown-ups, but if you've got a hot date lined up, I'm perfectly fine."

As she said the words, she tasted the lie in them. Was this weird ache in her stomach because she had been looking forward to the evening out—or because she didn't like the idea of him with a hot date?

"I don't have a date, hot or otherwise," he growled as he pulled the pickup and trailer to a stop next to a small paddock near the barn of the Brannon Ridge Ranch.

She eased back in the bench seat, a curious relief seeping through her. "Good. That's that. We can go together, just like always. It will be a fun night out for us."

Though she knew him well enough to know something was still on his mind, he said nothing as he pulled off his sunglasses and hooked them on the rearview mirror. What did his silence mean? Didn't he *want* to go with her?

"Faith," he began, but suddenly she didn't want to hear what he had to say.

"We'd better get the beautiful girl in your trailer unloaded before the kids get home."

She opened her door and jumped out before he could answer her. Yes, sometimes she was like her son, Barrett, who would rather hide out in his room all day and miss dinner than be scolded for something he'd done. She didn't like to face bad things. It was a normal reaction, she told herself. Hadn't she already had to face enough bad things in her life?

After a moment, Chase climbed out after her and came around to unhook the back of the trailer. The striking black-and-white paint yearling whinnied as he led her out into the patchy snow.

"She's a beauty, isn't she?" Faith said, struck all over again by the horse's elegant lines.

"Yeah," Chase said. Again with the monosyllables. She sighed.

"Thanks for letting me keep her here for a couple of weeks. Louisa will be so shocked on Christmas morning."

"Shouldn't be a problem."

He guided the horse into the pasture, where his own favorite horse, Tor, immediately trotted over as Faith closed the gate behind them. As soon as Chase unhooked the young horse from her lead line, she raced to the other side of the pasture, mane and tail flying out behind her.

She was fast. That was the truth. Grateful for her own cowboy hat that shielded her face from the worst of the frost-tipped snowflakes, Faith watched the horse race to the other corner of the pasture and back, obviously overflowing with energy after the stress of a day at the auction and then a trailer ride with strangers.

"Do you think she's too much horse for Lou?" she asked while Chase patted Tor beside her.

He looked at the paint and then down at Faith. "She comes from prime barrel racing stock. That's what Lou wants to do. For twelve, she's a strong rider. Yeah, the horse is only green broke but Seth Dalton can train a horse to do just about anything but recite its ABCs."

"I guess that's true. It was nice of him to agree to take her, with his crazy training schedule."

"He's a good friend."

"He is," she agreed. "Though I know he only agreed to do it as a favor to you."

"Maybe it was a favor to you," he commented as he pulled a bale of hay over and opened it inside the pasture for the horses.

"Maybe," she answered. All three Dalton brothers had been wonderful neighbors and good friends to her. They and others in the close-knit ranching community in Cold Creek Canyon and around Pine Gulch had stepped up in a hundred different ways over the last two and a half years since Travis died.

She would have been lost without any of them, but especially without Chase.

That vague unease slithered through her again. What was wrong between them? And how could she fix it?

She didn't have the first clue.

What was a guy supposed to do?

Ever since Beck McKinley cornered him at the diner to talk about taking Faith to the stockgrowers' holiday party, Chase hadn't been able to think straight. He felt like the other guy had grabbed his face and dunked it in an ice-cold water trough, then kicked him in the gut for good measure.

For a full ten seconds, he had stared at Beck as a host of emotions galloped through him faster than a pack of wild horses spooked by a thunderstorm.

Beckett McKinley wanted to date Faith. *Chase's* Faith.

"She's great. That's all," Beck had said into the suddenly tense silence. "It's been more than two years since Travis died, right? I just thought maybe she'd be ready to start getting out there."

Chase had thought for a minute his whole face had turned numb, especially his tongue. It made it tough for him to get any words out at all—or maybe that was the ice-cold coating around his brain.

"Why are you asking me?" he had finally managed to say.

If possible, Beck had looked even more uncomfortable. "The two of you are always together. Here at the auction, at the feed store, at the diner in town. I know you're neighbors and you've been friends for a long time. But if there's something more than that, I don't want to be an ass and step on toes. You don't have to tell me what happens to bulls who wander into somebody else's pen."

It was all he could do not to haul off and deck the guy for the implied comparison that Faith was just some lonely heifer, waiting for some smooth-talking bull to wander by.

Instead, he had managed to grip his hands into fists, all while one thought kept echoing through his head.

Not again.

He thought he was giving her time to grieve, to make room in her heart for someone else besides Travis Dustin, the man she had loved since she was a traumatized girl trying to carve out a new home for her and her sisters.

Chase had been too slow once before. He had been a steady friend and confidant from the beginning. He figured he had all the time in the world as he waited for her to heal and to settle into life in Pine Gulch. She had been so young, barely sixteen. He wasn't much older, not yet nineteen, and had been busy with his own struggles. Even then, he had been running his family's ranch on his own while his father lay dying.

For six months, he offered friendship to Faith, fully expecting that one day when both of them were in a better place, he could start moving things to a different level.

And then Travis Dustin came home for the summer

to help out Claude and Mary, the distant relatives who had raised him his last few years of high school.

Chase's father was in his last few agonizing weeks of life from lung cancer that summer. While he was busy coping with that and accepting his new responsibilities on the ranch, Travis had wasted no time sweeping in and stealing Faith's heart. By the time Chase woke up and realized what was happening, it was too late. His two closest friends were in love with each other and he couldn't do a damn thing about it.

He could have fought for her, he supposed, but it was clear from the beginning that Travis made her happy. After everything she and her sisters had been through, she deserved to find a little peace.

Instead, he had managed to put his feelings away and maintain his friendship with both of them. He had even tried to move on himself and date other women, with disastrous consequences.

Beck McKinley was a good guy. A solid rancher, a devoted father, a pillar of the community. Any woman would probably be very lucky to have him, as long as she could get past those hellion boys of his.

Maybe McKinley was exactly the kind of guy she wanted. The thought gnawed at him, but he took some small solace in remembering that she hadn't seemed all that enthusiastic at the idea of going out with him.

Didn't matter. He knew damn well it was only a matter of time before she found someone she *did* want to go out with. If not Beck, some other smooth-talking cowboy would sweep in.

He hadn't fought for her last time. Instead, he had

stood by like a damn statue and watched her fall in love with his best friend.

He wouldn't go through that again. It was time he made a move—but what if he made the wrong one and ruined everything between them?

He felt like a man given a choice between a hangman's noose and a firing squad. He was damned either way.

He was still trying to figure out what to do when she shifted from watching the young horse dance around the pasture in the cold December air. Faith gazed up at the overcast sky, still dribbling out the occasional stray snowflake.

"I probably should get back. The kids will be out of school soon and I'm sure you have plenty of things of your own to do. You don't have to walk me back," she said when he started to head in that direction behind her. "Stay and unhitch the horse trailer if you need to."

"It can keep. I'll walk you back up to your truck. I've got to plug in my phone anyway."

A couple of his ranch dogs came out from the barn to say hello as they walked the short distance to his house. He reached down and petted them both, in total sympathy. He felt like a ranch dog to her: a constant, steady companion with a few useful skills that came in handy once in a while.

Would she ever be able to see him as anything more?

"Thanks again, Chase," Faith said when they reached her own pickup truck—the one she had insisted on driving over that morning, even though he told her he could easily pick her up and drop her back off at the Star N.

"You're welcome," he said.

"Seriously, I was out of my depth. Horses aren't exactly my area of expertise. Who knows, I might have brought home a nag. As always, I don't know what I would do without you."

He could feel tension clutch at his shoulders again. "Not true," he said, his voice more abrupt than he intended. "You didn't need me. Not really. You'd already done your research and knew what you wanted in a barrel racer. You just needed somebody to back you up."

She smiled as they reached her pickup truck and a pale shaft of sunlight somehow managed to pierce the cloud cover and land right on her delicate features, so soft and lovely it made his heart hurt.

"I'm so lucky that somebody is always you," she said.

He let out a breath, fighting the urge to pull her into his arms. He didn't have that right—nor could he let things go on as they were.

"About the stockgrowers' party," he began.

If he hadn't been looking, he might have missed the leap of something that looked suspiciously like fear in her green eyes before she shifted her gaze away from him.

"Really, it doesn't bother me to skip it this year if you want to make other plans."

"I don't want to skip it," he growled. "I want to go. With you. On a date."

He intended to stress the last word, to make it plain this wouldn't be two buddies just hanging out together, like they always did. As a result, the word took on unnatural proportions and he nearly snapped it out until it arced between them like an arrow twanged from a crossbow.

Eyes wide, she gazed at him for a long moment, clearly startled by his vehemence. After a moment, she nodded. "Okay. That's settled, then. We can figure out the details later."

*Nothing* was settled. He needed to tell her *date* was the operative word here, that he didn't want to take her to the party as her neighbor and friend who gave her random advice on a barrel racing horse for her daughter or helped her with the hay season.

He wanted the right to hold her—to dance with her and flirt and whisper soft, sexy words in her ear.

How the hell could he tell her that, after all this time, when he had so carefully cultivated a safe, casual relationship that was the exact opposite of what he really wanted? Before he could figure that out, an SUV he didn't recognize drove up the lane toward his house.

"Were you expecting company?" she asked.

"Don't think so." He frowned as the car pulled up beside them—and his frown intensified when the passenger door opened and a girl jumped out, then raced toward him. "Daddy!"

## *Chapter Two*

He stared at his eleven-year-old daughter, dressed to the nines in an outfit more suited to a photo shoot for a children's clothing store than for a working cattle ranch.

"Adaline! What are you doing here? I didn't expect to see you until next weekend."

"I know, Dad! Isn't it great? We get extra time together—maybe even two whole weeks! Mom pulled me out of school until after Christmas. Isn't that awesome? My teachers are going to email me all my homework so I don't miss too much—not that they ever do anything the last few weeks before Christmas vacation anyway but waste time showing movies and doing busywork and stuff."

That sounded like a direct quote from her mother, who had little respect for the educational system, even the expensive private school she insisted on sending their daughter to.

As if on cue, his ex-wife climbed out of the driver's side of what must be a new vehicle, judging by the temporary license plates in the window.

She looked uncharacteristically disordered, with her sweater askew and her hair a little messy in back where she must have been leaning against the headrest as she drove.

"I'm so glad you're home," she said. "We took a chance. I've been trying to call you all afternoon. Why didn't you answer?"

"My phone ran out of juice and I forgot to take the charger to the auction with us. What's going on?"

He knew it had to be something dramatic for her to bring Addie all this way on an unscheduled mid-week visit.

Cindy frowned. "My mother had a stroke early this morning and she's in the hospital in Idaho Falls."

"Oh, no! I hadn't heard. I'm so sorry."

He had tried very hard to earn the approval of his in-laws but the president of the Pine Gulch bank and his wife had been very slow to warm up to him. He didn't know if they had disliked him because Cindy had been pregnant when they married or because they didn't think a cattle rancher with cow manure on his boots was good enough for their precious only child.

They had reached a peace accord of sorts after Addie came along. Still, he almost thought his and Cindy's divorce had been a relief to them—and he had no doubt they had been thrilled at her second marriage to an eminently successful oral surgeon in Boise.

"The doctors say it appears to be a mini stroke. They suspect it's not the first one so they want to keep her for observation for a few days. My dad said I didn't have to come down but it seemed like the right thing to do," Cindy said. "Considering I was coming this way anyway, I didn't think you would mind having extra visitation with Addie, especially since she won't be here over the holidays."

He was aware of a familiar pang in his chest, probably no different from what most part-time divorced fathers felt at not being able to live with their children all the time. Holidays were the worst.

"Sure. Extra time is always great."

Cindy turned to Faith with that hard look she always wore when she saw the two of them together. His ex-wife had never said anything but he suspected she had long guessed the feelings he had tried to bury after Faith and Travis got married.

"We're interrupting," she said. "I'm sorry."

"Not at all," Faith assured her. "Please don't be sorry. I'm the one who's sorry about your mother."

"Thanks," Cindy said, her voice cool. "We spent an hour at the hospital before we came out here and she seems in good spirits. Doctors just want to keep her for observation to see if they can figure out what's going on. Dad is kind of a mess right now, which is why I thought it would be a good idea for me to stay with him, at least for the first few days."

"That sounds like a good idea."

"Thanks for taking Addie. Sorry to drop her off without calling first. I did try."

"It's no problem at all. I'm thrilled to have her."

The sad truth was, they got along and seemed to parent together better now that they were divorced than during the difficult five years of their marriage, though things still weren't perfect.

"I packed enough for a week. To be honest, I don't know what I grabbed, since I was kind of a mess this morning. Keith was worried about me driving alone but he had three surgeries scheduled today and couldn't come with me. His patients needed him."

"He's a busy man," Chase said. What else *could* he say? It would have been terribly hypocritical to lambast another man in the husband department when Chase had been so very lousy at it.

"I should get back to the hospital. Thanks, Chase. You're a lifesaver."

"No problem."

"I'm so sorry about your mother," Faith said.

"Thank you. I appreciate that."

Cindy opened the hatchback of the SUV and pulled out Addie's familiar pink suitcase. He hated the tangible reminder that his daughter had to live out of a suitcase half her life.

After setting the suitcase on the sidewalk, Cindy went through her usual drawn-out farewell routine with Addie that ended in a big hug and a sloppy kiss, then climbed into her SUV and drove away.

"My feet are cold," Addie announced calmly, apparently not fazed at all to watch her mother leave, despite the requisite drama. "I'm going to take my suitcase to my room and change my clothes."

She headed to the house without waiting for him to answer, leaving him alone with Faith.

"That was a curveball I wasn't expecting this afternoon,"

"Strokes can be scary," Faith said. "It sounds like Carol's was a mild one, though, which I'm sure is a relief to everyone. At least you'll get to spend a little extra time with Addie."

"True. Always a bonus."

He had plenty of regrets about his life but his wise, funny, kind daughter was the one amazing thing his lousy marriage had produced.

"I know this was a busy week for you," Faith said. "If you need help with her, she's welcome to spend time at the Star N. Louisa would be completely thrilled."

He had appointments all week with suppliers, the vet and his accountant, but he could take her with him. She was a remarkably adaptable child.

"The only time I might need help is Friday night. Think Aunt Mary would mind if she stayed at your place with Lou and Barrett while we're at the party?"

Her forehead briefly furrowed in confusion. "Oh. I almost forgot about that. Look, the situation has changed. If you'd rather stay home with Addie, I completely understand. I can tag along with Wade and Caroline Dalton or Justin and Ashley Hartford. Or, again, I can always just skip it."

Was she looking for excuses not to go with him? He didn't want to believe that. "I asked you out. I want to go, as long as Mary doesn't mind one more at your place."

"Addie's never any trouble. I'm sure Mary will be fine with it. I'll talk to her," she promised. "If she can't do it, I'm sure all the kids could hang out with Hope or Celeste for the evening."

Her sisters and their husbands lived close to the Star N and often helped with Barrett and Louisa, just as Faith helped out with their respective children.

"I'll be in touch later in the week to work out the details."

"Sounds good." She glanced at her watch. "I really do need to go. Thanks again for your help with the horse."

"You're welcome."

As she climbed into the Star N king-cab pickup, he was struck by how small and delicate she looked compared to the big truck.

Physically, she might be slight—barely five-four and slender—but she was tough as nails. Over the last two and a half years, she had worked tirelessly to drag the ranch from the brink. He had tried to take some of the burden from her but there was only so much she would let him do.

He stepped forward so she couldn't close the door yet.

"One last thing."

"What's that?"

Heart pounding, he leaned in to face her. He wanted her to see his expression. He wanted no ambiguity about his intentions.

"You need to be clear on one thing before Friday. I said it earlier but in all the confusion with Addie show- ing up, I'm not sure it registered completely. As far as I'm concerned, this is a date."

"Sure. We're going together. What else would it be?"

"I mean a date-date. I want to go out with you where we're not only good friends hanging out on a Friday night or two neighboring ranchers carpooling to the same event. I want you to be my date, with everything that goes along with that."

There. She couldn't mistake *that*.

He saw a host of emotions quickly cross her features— shock, uncertainty and a wild flare of panic. "Chase, I—"

He could see she wasn't even going to give him a chance. She was ready to throw up barriers to the idea before he even had a chance. Frustration coiled through him, sharp as barbed wire fencing.

"It's been two and a half years since Travis died."

Her hands clamped tight onto the steering wheel as if it were a bull rider's strap and she had to hang on or she would fall off and be trampled. "Yes. I believe I'm fully aware of that."

"You're going to have to enter the dating scene at some point. You've already got cowboys clamoring to ask you out. McKinley is just the first one to step up, but he won't be the last. Why not ease into it by going out with somebody you already know?"

"You."

"Why not?"

Instead of answering, she turned the tables on him.

"You and Cindy have been divorced for years. Why are you suddenly interested in dating again?"

"Maybe I'm tired of being alone." That, at least, was the truth, just not the whole truth.

"So this would be like a…trial run for both of us? A way to dip our toes into the water without jumping in headfirst?"

No. He had jumped in a long, long time ago and had just been treading water, waiting for her.

He couldn't tell her that. Not yet.

"Sure, if you want to look at it that way," he said instead.

He knew her well enough that he could almost watch her brain whir as she tried to think through all the ram-ifications. She overthought everything. It was by turns endearing and endlessly frustrating.

Finally she seemed to have sifted through the possi-bilities and come up with a scenario she could live with. "You're such a good friend, Chase. You've always got my back. You want to help make this easier for me, just like you helped me buy the horse for Louisa. Thank you."

He opened his mouth to say that wasn't at all his in-tention but he could see by the stubborn set of her jaw that she wasn't ready to hear that yet.

"I'll talk to Aunt Mary about keeping an eye on the kids on Friday. We can work out the details later. I re-ally do have to go. Thanks again."

Her tone was clearly dismissive. Left with no real choice, he stepped back so she could close the vehicle door.

She was deliberately misunderstanding him and he

didn't know how to argue with her. After all these years of being her friend and so carefully hiding his feelings, how did he convince her he wanted to be more than that?

He had no idea. He only knew he had to try.

Faith refused to let herself panic.

*I want you to be my date, with everything that goes along with that.*

Despite her best efforts, fear seemed to curl around her insides, coating everything with a thin layer of ice.

She couldn't let things change. End of story. Chase had been her rock for two years, her best friend, the one constant in her crazy, tumultuous life. He had been the first one she had called when she had gone looking for Travis after he didn't answer his cell and found him unconscious and near death, with severe internal injuries and a shattered spine, next to his overturned ATV.

Chase had been there within five minutes and had taken charge of the scene, had called the medics and the helicopter, had been there at the hospital and had held her after the doctors came out with their solemn faces and their sad eyes.

While she had been numb and broken, Chase had stepped in, organizing all the neighbors to bring in the fall harvest. He had helped her clean up and streamline the Star N operation and sell off all the unnecessary stock to keep their head above water those first few months.

Now the ranch was in the black again—thanks in large part to the crash course in smart ranch practices

Chase had given her. She knew perfectly well that without him, there wouldn't *be* a Star N right now or The Christmas Ranch. She and her sisters would have had to sell off the land, the cattle, *everything* to pay their debts.

Travis hadn't been a very good businessman. At his death, she'd found the ranch was seriously overextended with creditors and had been operating under a system of gross inefficiencies for years.

She winced with the guilt the disloyal thought always stirred in her, but it was nothing less than the truth. If her husband hadn't died and things had continued on the same course, the ranch would have gone bankrupt within a few years. Through Chase's extensive help, she had been able to turn things around.

The ranch was doing so much better. The Christmas Ranch—the seasonal attraction started by her uncle and aunt after she and her sisters came to live with them—was finally in the black, too. Hope and her husband, Rafe, had done an amazing job revitalizing it and making it a powerful draw. That success had only been augmented by the wild viral popularity of the charming children's book Celeste had written and Hope had illustrated featuring the ranch's starring attraction, Sparkle the Reindeer.

She couldn't be more proud of her sisters—though she did find it funny that, of the three of them, *Faith* seemed the one most excited that Celeste and Hope had signed an agreement to allow a production company to make an animated movie out of the first Sparkle book.

Despite a few preproduction problems, the process

was currently under way, though the animated movie wouldn't come out for another year. The buzz around it only heightened interest in The Christmas Ranch and led to increased revenue.

The book had helped push The Christmas Ranch to self-sufficiency. Without that steady drain on the Star N side of the family operation, Faith had been able to plow profits back into the cattle ranch operation.

As she drove past the Saint Nicholas Lodge on the way to the ranch house, she spotted both of her sisters' vehicles in the parking lot.

After taking up most of the day at the auction, she had a hundred things to do. As she had told Chase, Barrett and Louisa would be home from school soon. When she could swing it, she liked being there to greet them, to ask about their day and help manage their homework and chore responsibilities.

On a whim, though, she pulled into the parking lot and hurriedly texted both of her children as well as Aunt Mary to tell them she was stopping at the lodge for a moment and would be home soon.

The urge to talk to her sisters was suddenly overwhelming. Hope and Celeste weren't just her sisters, they were her best friends.

She had to park three rows back, which she considered a great sign for a Tuesday afternoon in mid-December.

Tourists from as far away as Boise and Salt Lake City were making the trek here to visit their quaint little Christmas attraction, with its sleigh rides, the reindeer herd, the village—and especially because this was the home of Sparkle.

As far as she was concerned, this was just home.

The familiar scents inside the lodge encircled her the moment she walked inside—cinnamon and vanilla and pine, mixed with old logs and the musty smell of a building that stood empty most of the year.

She heard her younger sisters bickering in the office before she saw them.

"Cry your sad song to someone else," Celeste was saying. "I told you I wasn't going to do it again this year and I won't let you guilt me into it."

"But you did such a great job last year," Hope protested.

"Yes I did," their youngest sister said. "And I swore I wouldn't ever do it again."

Faith poked her head into the office in time to see Hope pout. She was nearly three months pregnant and only just beginning to show.

"It didn't turn out so badly," Hope pointed out. "You ended up with a fabulous husband and a new stepdaughter out of the deal, didn't you?"

"Seriously? You're giving the children's show credit for my marriage to Flynn?"

"Think about it. Would you be married to your hunky contractor right now and deliriously happy if you hadn't directed the show for me last year—and if his daughter hadn't begged to participate?"

It was an excellent point, Faith thought with inward amusement that Celeste didn't appear to share.

"Why can't you do it?" Celeste demanded.

"We are booked solid with tour groups at the ranch until Christmas Eve. I won't have a minute to breathe from now until the New Year—and that's with Rafe making me cut down my hours."

"You knew you were going to be slammed," Celeste said, not at all persuaded. "Talk about procrastination. I can't believe you didn't find somebody to organize the variety show weeks ago!"

"I *had* somebody. Linda Keller told me clear back in September she would do it. I thought we were set, but she fell this morning and broke her arm, which leaves me back at square one. The kids are going to be coming to practice a week from today and I've got absolutely no one to lead them."

Hope shifted her attention to Faith with a considering look that struck fear in her heart.

"Oh, no," she exclaimed. "You can forget that idea right now."

"Why?" Hope pouted. "You love kids and senior citizens both, plus you sing like a dream. You even used to direct the choir at church, which I say makes you the perfect one to run the Christmas show."

She rolled her eyes. Hope knew better than to seriously consider that idea. "Right. Because you know I've got absolutely nothing else going on right now."

"Everyone is busy. That's the problem. Whose idea was it to put on a show at Christmas, the busiest time of the year?"

"Yours." Faith and Celeste answered simultaneously.

Hope sighed. "I know. It just seemed natural for The Christmas Ranch to throw a holiday celebration for the senior citizens. Maybe next year we'll do a Christmas in July kind of thing."

"Except you'll be having a baby in July," Faith pointed out. "And I'll be even more busy during the summer."

"You're right." She looked glum. "Do you have any suggestions for someone else who might be interested in directing it? I would hate to see the pageant fade out, especially after last year was such a smash success, thanks to CeCe. You wouldn't believe how many people have stopped me in town during the past year to tell me how much they enjoyed it and hoped we were doing another one."

"I believe it," Celeste said. "I've had my share of people telling me the same thing. That still doesn't mean I want to run it again."

"I wasn't even involved with the show and I still have people stop me in town to tell me they hope we're doing it again," Faith offered.

"That's because you're a Nichols," Hope said.

"Right. Which to some people automatically means I burp tinsel and have eggnog running through my veins."

Celeste laughed. "You don't?"

"Nope. Hope inherited all the Christmas spirit from Uncle Claude and Aunt Mary."

The sister in question made a face. "That may be true, but it still doesn't give me someone to run the show this year. But never fear. I've got a few ideas up my sleeves."

"I can help," Celeste said. "I just don't want to be the one in charge."

Faith couldn't let her younger sister be the only generous one in the family. She sighed. "Okay. I'll help again, too. But only behind the scenes—and only because you're pregnant and I don't want you to overdo."

Hope's eyes glittered and her smile wobbled. "Oh. You're both going to make me cry and Rafe tells me I've already hit my tear quota for the day. Quick, talk about something else. How did the auction go today?"

At the question, all her angst about Chase flooded back.

She suddenly desperately wanted to confide in her sisters. That was the whole reason she'd stopped at the lodge, she realized, because she yearned to share this startling development with them and obtain their advice.

*I want you to be my date, with everything that goes along with that.*

What was she going to do?

She wanted to ask them but they both adored Chase and it suddenly seemed wrong to talk about him with Hope and Celeste. If she had to guess, she expected they would probably take his side. They wouldn't understand how he had just upended everything safe and secure she had come to depend upon.

When she didn't answer right away, both of her sisters looked at her with concern. "Did something go wrong with the horse you wanted to buy?" Celeste asked. "You weren't outbid, were you? If you were, I'm sure you'll be able to find another one."

She shook her head. "No. We bought the horse for about five percent under what I was expecting to pay and she's beautiful. Mostly white with black spots and lovely black boot markings on her legs. I can't wait for Louisa to see her."

"I want to see her!" Hope said. "You took her to Chase's pasture?"

"Yes, and a few moments after we unloaded her, Cindy pulled up with Addie. Apparently Carol Johnson had a small stroke this morning and she's in the hospital in Idaho Falls so Cindy came home to be with her and help her father."

At the mention of Chase's ex-wife, both of her sisters' mouths tightened in almost exactly the same way. There had been no love lost between any of them, especially after Cindy's affair with the oral surgeon who eventually became her husband.

"So Cindy just dropped off Addie like UPS delivering a surprise package?" Hope asked, disgust clear in her voice.

"What about school?" ever-practical Celeste asked. "Surely she's not out for Christmas break yet."

"No. She's going to do her homework from here." She paused, remembering the one other complication. "I haven't asked Mary yet if she's available but in case she's not, would either of you like a couple of extra kids on Friday night? Three, actually—my two and Addie. Chase and I have a…a thing and it might run late."

"Oh, I wish I could," Hope exclaimed. "Rafe and I promised Joey we would take him to Boise to see his mom. We're staying overnight and doing some shopping while we're there."

"How is Cami doing?" Faith asked. "She's been out of prison, what, three months now?"

"Ten weeks. She's doing so well. Much better than Rafe expected, really. The court-ordered drug rehab she had in prison worked in her case and the halfway house is really helping her get back on her feet. Another six months and she's hoping she can have her own place and be ready to take Joey back. Maybe even by the time the baby comes."

Hope tried to smile but it didn't quite reach her eyes and Faith couldn't resist giving her sister's hand a squeeze. Celeste did the same to the other hand. Hope and her husband had cared for Rafe's nephew Joey since before their marriage after his sister's conviction on drug and robbery charges. They loved him and would both be sad to see him go.

Joey seemed like a different kid than he'd been when he first showed up at The Christmas Ranch with Rafe, two years earlier, sullen and confused and angry...

"We're trying to convince her to come back to Pine Gulch," Hope said, trying to smile. "It might help her stay out of trouble, and that way we can remain part of Joey's life. So far it's an uphill battle, as she feels like this is where all her troubles started."

Her sister's turmoil was a sharp reminder to Faith. Hope might be losing the boy she considered a son, and Celeste's stepdaughter, Olivia, still struggled to recover from both physical injuries and the emotional trauma of witnessing her mother's murder at the hands of her mentally ill and suicidal boyfriend.

In contrast, the problem of trying to figure out what to do with Chase seemed much more manageable.

"Anyway," Hope said, "that's why I won't be around Friday to help you with the kids. Sorry again."

"Don't give it another thought. That's exactly where you need to be."

"The kids are more than welcome at our place," Celeste said. "Flynn and Olivia are having a movie marathon and watching *Miracle on 34th Street* and *White Christmas*. I'll be writing during most of it, but hope to sneak in and watch the dancing in *White Christmas*."

She used to love those movies, Faith remembered. When she was young, her parents had a handful of very old, very worn VCR tapes of several holiday classics and would drag them from place to place, sometimes even showing them at social events for people in whatever small village they had set their latest medical clinic in at the time.

She probably had been just as baffled as the villagers at the world shown in the movies, which seemed so completely foreign to her own life experience, with the handsomely dressed people and the luxurious train rides and the children surrounded by toys she could only imagine.

"That sounds like the perfect evening," she said now. "Maybe I'll join the movie night instead of going to a boring Christmas party with Chase. I can bring the popcorn."

"You can't skip the stockgrowers' party," Celeste said. "It's the big social event of the year, isn't it? Jenna McRaven always caters that gala so you know the food will be fantastic, plus you'll be going with Chase. How can any party be boring with him around?"

Again, she wanted to blurt out to her sisters how strangely he was acting. She even opened her mouth to do it but before she could force the words out, she heard familiar young voices outside in the hallway just an instant before Barrett and Louisa poked their heads in, followed in short order by Celeste's stepdaughter, Olivia, and Joey. Liv went straight to Celeste while Joey practically jumped into Hope's outstretched arms.

It warmed her heart so much to see her sisters being such loving mother figures to children who needed them desperately.

"Joey and Olivia were coming to the house to hang out when I got your text," Louisa said. "We saw all your cars so decided to stop here to say hi before we walk up to the house from the bus stop."

"I'm so glad you did," Faith said.

She hugged them both, her heart aching with love. "Good day?" she asked.

Louisa nodded. "Pretty good. I had a substitute for science and she was way nicer than Mr. Lewis."

"Guess who got a hundred-ten percent on his math test?" Barrett said with a huge grin "Go on. Guess."

She made a big show of looking confused and glancing in the other boy's direction. "You did, Joey? Good job, kid!"

Rafe's nephew giggled. "I only got a hundred percent. I missed the extra credit but Barrett didn't."

Her son preened. "I was the only one in the class who got it right."

"I'm proud of both of you. What a smart family we have!"

Except for her, the one who couldn't figure out how to protect the friendship that meant the world to her.

## Chapter Three

As he drove up to the Star N ranch house four days after the auction, Chase couldn't remember the last time he'd been so on edge. He wasn't nervous—or at least he would never admit to it. He was just unsettled.

So many things seemed to hinge on this night. How was he supposed to make Faith ever view him as more than just her neighbor and best friend? She had to see him for himself, a man who had spent nearly half his life waiting for her.

He didn't like the way that made him sound weak, like some kind of mongrel hanging on the fringes of her life, content for whatever scraps she threw out the kitchen door at him. It hadn't been like that. He had genuinely tried to put his unrequited feelings behind him after she and Travis got married. For the most part, he had succeeded.

He had dated a great deal and had genuinely liked several of the women he dated. In the beginning, he had liked Cindy, too. She had been funny and smart and beautiful. He was a man and had been flattered— and susceptible—when she aggressively pursued him.

When she told him she was pregnant, he decided marrying her and making a home for their child was the right thing to do. He really had tried to make their marriage work but he and Cindy were a horrible mismatch from the beginning. He could see now that they would never have suited each other, even if that little dusty corner of his heart hadn't belonged to the wife of another man.

"This is going to be so fun," Addie declared beside him. She was just about dancing out of her seat belt with excitement. "Seems like it's been forever since I've had a chance to hang out with Louisa and Olivia. It's going to be awesome."

The plan for the evening had changed at the last minute, Faith had told him in a quick, rather awkward conversation earlier that day. Celeste and Flynn decided to move their movie party to the Star N ranch house and the three girls were going to stay overnight after the movie.

If Lou and Olivia were as excited as Addie, Celeste and Mary were in for a night full of giggling girls.

His daughter let out a little shriek when he pulled up and turned off the engine.

"This is going to be *so fun!*" she repeated.

He had to smile as he climbed out and walked around to open the door. He never got tired of seeing the joy his daughter found in the simple things in life.

"Hand me your suitcase."

"Here. You don't have to carry everything, though. I can take the rest."

After pulling her suitcase from behind the seat, she hopped out with her pillow and sleeping bag.

"Careful. It's icy," he said as they headed up the sidewalk to the sprawling ranch house.

She sent him an appraising look as they reached the front door. "You look really good, Dad," she declared. "Like, Nick Jonas good."

"That's quite a compliment." Or it would be if he had more than the vaguest idea who Nick Jonas was.

"It's true. I bet you'll be the hottest guy at the party, especially since everyone else will be a bunch of married old dudes, right?"

He wasn't sure about that. Justin Hartford was a famous—though retired—movie star and Seth Dalton had once been quite a lady's man in these parts.

"You're sweet, kiddo," he said, kissing the top of her head that smelled like grape-scented shampoo.

Man, he loved this kid and missed her like crazy when she was staying with her mother.

"Doesn't their house look pretty?" she said cheerfully as she rang the doorbell.

The Star N ranch house was ablaze with multicolored Christmas lights around the windows and along the roofline, and their Christmas tree glowed merrily in the front bay window.

It was warm and welcoming against the cold, starry night.

The first year after Travis died, Faith had refused to hang any outside Christmas lights on the house and had only had a Christmas tree because Chase had decorated her Christmas tree with the kids and Aunt Mary. Faith hadn't been up to it and had claimed ranch business elsewhere while they did it.

Last year, he and Rafe had hung the outside Christmas lights.

This year, Faith herself had hung the lights, with Barrett and Lou helping her.

He wanted to think there was some symbolism in that, one more example that she was moving forward with her life.

Addie was about to ring the doorbell again when it suddenly opened. Faith's aunt stood on the other side and at the sight of him, Mary gave a low, appreciative whistle that made him feel extremely self-conscious.

"I should yell at you for ringing the doorbell when I've told you a hundred times you're family, but you look so good, I was about to ask Miss Addie what handsome stranger brought her to our door."

His daughter giggled and kissed the wrinkled cheek Mary offered. "Hi, Aunt Mary. It's just my dad. But I told him on the way that he looked super hot. For an old guy, anyway."

He *felt* hot in his suit and tie, but probably not the way she meant. Mary grinned. "You're absolutely right," she said. "Nice to see you dressed up for once."

"Thanks," he answered.

Before he could say more, Louisa burst into the room and started dancing around Addie. "You're here! You're here! I've been dying to see you and do more than just talk on the phone and text and stuff. It feels like *forever* since you've been here."

The girls hugged as if they had been separated for months.

"Need me to carry your stuff to your room?" he asked.

"It's just a suitcase and sleeping bag, Dad. I think we can handle it."

"Let's hurry, before Barrett finds out you're here and starts bugging us," Louisa said.

Poor Barrett, who until recently had been completely outnumbered by all the women in his life. At least now he had a couple of uncles and an honorary cousin in Rafe's nephew, Joey.

"Faith only came in from the barn about half an hour ago so she's still getting ready," Mary said, her plump features tight with disapproval for a moment before she wiped the expression away and gave him a smile instead. "I heard the shower turn off a few minutes ago so it shouldn't be long now."

He tried not to picture Faith climbing out of the shower, all creamy skin with her tight, slender body covered in water droplets. Once the image bloomed there, it was tough to get it out of his head again to focus on anything else.

"It's fine," he answered. "We've got plenty of time."

"You're too patient," Mary said. Her voice had an unusually barbed tone to it that made him think she wasn't necessarily talking about him waiting for Faith to get dressed for their night out.

"Maybe I just don't want to make anybody feel rushed," he answered carefully—also talking about more than just that evening.

Mary sniffed. "That's all well and good, but sometimes time can be your worst enemy, son. People get set in their ways and can't see the world is still brimming over with possibilities. Sometimes they need a sharp boot in the keister to point them in the right direction."

Well, that was clear enough. Mary *definitely* wasn't talking about the time Faith was taking to get ready. He gave her a searching look. Maybe he hadn't been as careful as he thought about not wearing his heart on his sleeve.

He loved Faith's aunt, who had opened her home and her heart to Faith and her sisters after the horrible events before they came to Pine Gulch. She and Claude had offered a safe haven for three grieving girls but they had provided much more than that. Through steady love and care, the couple had helped the girls begin to heal.

Mary had truly been a lifesaver after Travis's death, as well. She had moved back into the ranch house and stepped up to help with the children while Faith struggled to juggle widowhood and single motherhood while suddenly saddled with the responsibilities of running a big cattle ranch on her own.

"I'm just saying," Mary went on, "maybe it's time to get off your duff and make a move."

He could feel tension spread out from his head to

his shoulders. "That's the plan. What do you think to-night is about?"

"I was hoping."

She frowned, blue eyes troubled. "Just between me and you and that Christmas tree, I've got a feeling that might be the reason why a certain person just came in from the barn only a half hour ago, even though she knew all day you were on the way and exactly what time she would need to start getting ready."

Did that mean Mary thought Faith was avoiding the idea of going on a real date with him? He couldn't tell and before he had the chance to ask for clarification, Flynn Delaney came into the living room.

The other man did a double take when he spotted Chase talking to Mary. "Wow. A tie and everything."

Chase shrugged, though he could feel his skin prickle. "A Christmas party for the local stockgrowers association might not be a red-carpet Hollywood affair, but it's still a pretty big deal around here."

"Take it from me—it will be much more enjoyable for everyone involved."

He wasn't so sure about that, especially if Faith was showing reluctance about the evening.

"Sometime this week, Rafe and I are planning to spruce up the set we used last year for the Christmas show. If you want to lend a hand, we'll pay you in beer."

He had come to truly enjoy the company of both of Faith's brothers-in-law. They were both decent men who, as far as he was concerned, were almost good enough for her sisters.

"Addie's in town right now and I feel bad enough

about leaving her tonight when our time together is limited. I'll have to see what she wants to do but I'm sure she wouldn't mind coming out again and riding horses with Lou."

"I get it. Believe me."

Flynn had been a divorced father, too. He and his famous actress wife had been divorced several years before she was eventually killed so tragically.

The other man looked down the hallway, apparently to make sure none of the kids were in earshot. "I hear a certain *H-O-R-S-E* is safely ensconced at your place now."

"Lou is twelve years old and can spell, you know," Mary said with a snort.

Flynn grinned at the older woman. "Yeah. But will she slow down long enough to bother taking time to do it? That's the question."

Chase had to laugh. The horse and Louisa would be perfect for each other. "Yeah. She's a beauty. Louisa is going to be thrilled, I think. You all are in for a fun Christmas morning."

"You'll come over for breakfast like you usually do, won't you?" Mary asked.

He wasn't so sure about that. Maybe he would have to see how that evening went first. He hoped like hell that he wasn't about to ruin all his most important relationships with Faith's family by muddying the water with her.

"I hope so," he started to say, but the words died when he heard a commotion on the stairs and a moment later, Faith hurried down them wearing a silver-and-blue dress that made her look like a snow princess.

"Sorry. I'm so sorry I'm late," Faith exclaimed as she fastened a dangly silver earring.

He couldn't have responded, since his brain seemed to have shut down.

She looked absolutely stunning, with her hair piled on top of her head in a messy, sexy bun, strands artfully escaping in delectable ways. She wore a rosy lipstick and more eye makeup than usual, with mascara and eyeliner that made her eyes look huge and exotically slanted.

The dress hugged her shape, with a neckline that revealed just a hint of cleavage. She wore strappy sandals that made him wonder if he was going to have to scoop her up and carry her through the snow.

He was so used to seeing her in jeans and a T-shirt and boots, wearing a ponytail and little makeup except lip balm.

She was beautiful either way.

He swallowed, realizing he had to say something and not just stand there like an idiot.

"You're worth the wait," he said.

His voice came out rough and she flashed him a startled look before he saw color climb her cheeks.

"I don't know about that. It's been a crazy day and I feel like I've been running since five a.m. I'll probably fall asleep the moment I get into your truck."

He would love to have her curl up beside him and sleep. It certainly wouldn't be the first time.

"I'll have to see what I can do to keep you awake," he murmured.

"Driving with the windows down and the music cranked always helps me," Flynn offered.

"I spent too long fixing that hair for you to mess it up with a wind tunnel," Celeste Nichols Delaney said as she followed her sister down the stairs.

Her words brought Chase to his senses and he realized he had been standing in the entryway, gaping at her like he'd never seen a beautiful woman before.

He cleared his throat and forced himself to smile at Celeste. "We can't have that. You did a great job."

"I did, especially with Faith trying to send three emails, put on her makeup and help Barrett with his English homework at the same time."

"I appreciate your hard work," Faith said. "I think I'm finally ready. I just need my coat."

She made it the rest of the way down the stairs on the high heels and reached inside the closet in the entryway, but before she could pull off the serviceable ranch coat she always wore, Celeste slapped her hand away. "Oh, no you don't."

Faith frowned at her sister. "Why not? This is a stockgrowers' dinner. You think they've never seen a ranch coat before?"

"Not with that dress, they haven't. That's why I brought over this."

She pulled a soft fawn coat reverently from the arm of the sofa. "I bought this last month in New York when Hope and I were there meeting with our publisher."

"I don't want to wear your fancy coat."

"Too bad. You're going to."

Celeste could be as stubborn as the other sisters. "Fine," Faith finally sighed, reaching for the coat that looked cashmere and expensive. With a subtle wink, Celeste ignored her sister's outstretched hand and gave it to Chase instead. It was soft as a newborn kitten. He felt inordinately breathless as he moved behind Faith and helped her into it.

She smelled…different. Usually she smelled of vanilla and oranges from her favorite soap but this was a little more intense, with a low, flowery note that made him want to bury his face in her neck and inhale.

"There you go," he said gruffly.

"Thanks." It was obvious she wasn't comfortable dressing up, perhaps because so much of her childhood was spent with parents who gave away most of their material possessions to the people they worked with in impoverished countries.

"Are you happy now?" Faith said to her sister.

"Yes. You're beautiful." Celeste's eyes were soft and a little teary. "Sometimes you look so much like Mom."

"She must have been stunning," Flynn said, kissing his sister-in-law on the cheek.

Chase cleared away the little catch in his throat. "Breathtaking," he agreed.

Her cheeks turned pink at the attention. "I still think we'd have much more fun staying home and watching Christmas movies with the kids," she said. She smiled at the three of them but he was almost certain he saw a flicker of nervousness in her eyes again.

"Now, there's absolutely no reason for the two of

you to rush back," Celeste assured them. "The three of us have got this covered. The kids will all be fine. Go and have a great time."

"That's right," Mary said. She gave Chase a pointed look, as if to remind him of their conversation earlier. "You ask me, these parties end way too soon. I suppose that's what you get when you hang out with people who have to wake up early to feed their livestock. So don't feel like you have to come straight home when it's over. You could even go catch a movie in town if you wanted or grab drinks at that fancy new bar that opened up on the outskirts of town."

"The only trouble is we both *also* have to wake up early to take care of our livestock," Faith said with a laugh that sounded slightly strained.

"Louisa. Barrett," she called. "I'm leaving. Come give me a hug."

All the children, not only her two, hurried down the stairs to join them.

"You look beautiful, Faith," Addie exclaimed. "What a cute couple you guys are. Wait. Let me get a picture so I can show my friends."

She pulled out the smartphone he didn't think she needed yet and snapped a picture.

"Oh! What a good idea," Celeste said. "I want a picture, too."

"We're just going to a Christmas party. It's not the prom," Faith said. Her color ratcheted up a notch, especially when Aunt Mary pulled out her phone as well and started clicking away taking pictures.

"I'm posting this one," her aunt declared. "You both

look so good. In fact, you better watch it, Chase, or you'll have about a hundred marriage proposals before the night is over. My friends on social media can be a wild bunch."

Faith's cheeks by now were as red as the ornaments on the tree. This was distressing her, and though he didn't quite understand why, it didn't matter. His job was to protect her—even from loving relatives with cell phone cameras.

"Okay, that's enough paparazzi for tonight. We'll really be late if this keeps up."

"You don't want that. You'll miss all of Jenna McRaven's good food," Mary said.

"Exactly." He hugged his daughter. "Be good, Ads. I imagine you'll still be up when I bring Faith back but if you're not, I'll see you in the morning."

"Bye, Dad. Have fun."

He waited for Faith to hug and kiss her kids and admonish them to behave for Aunt Mary and the Delaneys, then he held the door open for her and they headed out into the cold air that felt refreshing on his overheated skin.

Neither of them said anything as he led her to his pickup and helped her inside. He wished he had some kind of luxury sedan to take her to the party but that kind of vehicle wasn't very practical on an eastern Idaho ranch. At least he'd taken the truck for a wash and had vacuumed up any dried mud and straw bits out of the inside.

It took a little effort to tuck the soft length of her coat inside. "Better make sure I don't shut the door on

Celeste's coat," he joked. "She would probably never forgive me."

He went around and climbed inside, then turned his pickup truck around and started heading toward the canyon road that would take them to Pine Gulch and the party.

"My family. Ugh. You'd think I never went to a Christmas party before, the way they carry on." Faith didn't look at him as she fiddled with the air vent. "I don't know what's gotten into them all. I mean, we went together last year to the exact same party and nobody gave it a second thought."

A wise man would probably keep his mouth shut, just go with the flow.

Maybe he was tired of keeping his mouth shut.

"If I had to guess," he said, after giving her a long look, "they're making a fuss because they know this is different, that we're finally going out on a real date."

## Chapter Four

At his words, tension seemed to clamp around her spine with icy fingers.

*We're finally going out on a real date.*

She had really been hoping he had forgotten all that nonsense by now and they could go to the party as they always had done things, as dear friends.

She didn't know what to say. She couldn't stop thinking about that moment when she had started down the stairs and had seen him standing there, looking tall and rugged and gorgeous, freshly shaved and wearing a dark Western-cut suit and tie.

He had looked like he should be going to a country music awards show with a beautiful starlet on his arm or something, not the silly local stockgrowers association party with *her*.

She had barely been able to think straight and literally had felt so weak-kneed she considered it a minor miracle that she hadn't stumbled down the stairs right at his feet.

Then he had spotted her and the heat in his eyes had sent an entire flock of butterflies swarming through her insides.

"Every time I bring up that this is a date, you go silent as dirt," he murmured. "Why is that?"

She drew in a breath. "I don't know what to say."

He shot her a quick look across the bench seat of his truck. "Is the idea of dating me so incomprehensible?"

"Not incomprehensible. Just...disconcerting," she answered honestly.

"Why?" he pressed.

How was she supposed to answer that? He was her best friend and knew all her weaknesses and faults. Surely he knew she was a giant coward at heart, that she didn't *want* these new and terrifying feelings.

She had no idea how to answer him so she opted to change the subject. "I haven't had a chance to ask you. How's Louisa's new horse?"

He shifted his gaze from the road, this time to give her a long look. She thought for a moment he would call her on it and press for an answer. To her relief, he turned back to the road and, after a long pause, finally answered her.

"Settling in, I guess. She seems to have really taken to Tor—and vice versa."

"I hope they won't be too upset at being separated

when we send the new horse to Seth Dalton's after Christmas."

"I'm sure they'll survive. If not, we can always arrange visitation."

That word inevitably reminded her of his ex-wife.

"How is Cindy's mother doing?" she asked.

He shrugged. "Fine, from what I hear. She's probably going to be in the hospital another week."

"Does that mean the cruise is off?"

"Cindy insists they don't want to cancel the cruise unless it's absolutely necessary. I'm still planning my Christmas celebration with Addie on December 20."

"It's just another day on the calendar," she said.

"Don't let Hope hear you say that or she might ban you from The Christmas Ranch," he joked.

They spoke of the upcoming children's Christmas show and the crowds at the ranch and the progress of her sisters' movie for the remainder of the short drive to the reception hall where the annual dinner and party was always held.

He found a parking space not far from the building and climbed out to walk around the vehicle to her side. While she waited for him to open her door, Faith took a deep breath.

She could do this. Tonight was no different from dozens of other social events they had attended together. Weddings, birthday parties, Fourth of July barbecues. Things had never been awkward between them until now.

*We're finally going out on a real date.*

When she thought of those words, little starbursts of panic flared inside her.

She couldn't give in. Chase was her dear friend and she cared about him deeply. As long as she kept that in mind, everything would be just fine.

She wasn't certain she completely believed that but she refused to consider the alternative right now.

The party was in full swing when they arrived. The reception hall had been decorated with an abundance of twinkling fairy lights strung end to end and Christmas trees stood in each corner. Delectable smells wafted out of the kitchen and her stomach growled, almost in time to the band playing a bluegrass version of "Good King Wenceslas." A few couples were even dancing and she watched them with no small amount of envy. She missed dancing.

"You'd better give me Celeste's New York City coat so I can hang it up," Chase said from beside her.

She gave him a rueful smile. "I'm a little afraid to let it out of my sight but I guess I can't wear it all night."

"No, you can't. Go on inside. I'll hang this and be there in a moment."

She nodded and stepped into the reception room. Her good friend Jennie Dalton—Seth Dalton's wife and principal of the elementary school—stood just inside. Jennie was talking with Ashley Hartford, who taught kindergarten at the elementary school.

While their husbands were lost in conversation, the two women were speaking with a young, lovely woman she didn't recognize—which was odd, since she knew just about everyone who came to these events.

Jennie held out a hand when she spotted her. "Hello, my dear. You look gorgeous, as always."

Faith made a face, wishing she didn't feel like a frazzled, overburdened rancher and single mother.

She held a hand out to the woman she didn't know. "Hi. I'm Faith Dustin."

The woman had pretty features and a sweet smile. "Hello. I'm Ella Baker. You may know my father, Curt."

"Yes, of course. Hello. Lovely to meet you."

Curt Baker had a ranch on the other side of town. She didn't know him well but she had heard he had a daughter he didn't know well who had spent most of her life living with her mother back East somewhere. From what she understood, his daughter had returned to help him through a health scare.

"Your dad is looking well."

Ella glanced at her father with a troubled look, then forced a smile. "He's doing better, I suppose."

"Ella is a music therapist and she just agreed to take the job of music teacher at the school for the rest of the school year," Jennie said, looking thrilled at the prospect.

"That's a long time coming."

"Right. We've had the funding for it but haven't been able to find someone suitable since Linda Keller retired two years ago. We've been relying on parent volunteers, who have been wonderful, but can only take the program so far. I'm a firm believer that children learn better when we can incorporate the arts in the classroom."

"I completely agree," Faith said, then was suddenly struck by a small moment of brilliance. "Hey, I've got a terrific way for you to get to know some of the young people in the community."

"Oh?"

"My family runs The Christmas Ranch. You may have seen signs for it around town."

"Absolutely. I haven't had time to stop yet but it looks utterly delightful."

"It is." She didn't bother telling the woman she had very little to do with the actual operations of The Christmas Ranch. It was always too complicated explaining that she ran the cattle side of things—hence her presence at this particular holiday party.

"Last year we started a new tradition of offering a children's Christmas variety show and dinner for the senior citizens in town. It's nothing grand, more for fun than anything else. The children only practice for the week leading up to the show, since everyone is so busy this time of year. Linda Keller, the woman who retired a few years ago from the school district, had offered to help us this year but apparently she just broke her arm."

"That's as good an excuse as any," Ashley said.

"I suppose. The point is my sisters are desperate for someone to help them organize the show. I don't suppose there's any chance you might be interested."

It seemed a nervy thing to ask a woman she had only met five minutes earlier. To Faith's relief, Ella Baker didn't seem offended.

"That sounds like a blast," Ella exclaimed. "I've been looking for something to keep me busy until the New Year when I start at the school part-time."

Hope was going to owe her *big-time*—so much that Faith might even claim naming rights over the new baby.

"Great! You'll have fun, I promise. The kids are so cute and we've got some real talent."

"This is true," Ashley said. "Especially Faith's niece, Olivia. She sings like an angel. Last year the show was so wonderful."

"The senior citizens in the area really ate it up," Jennie affirmed. "My dad couldn't stop talking about it. The Nichols family has started a wonderful thing for the community."

"This sounds like a great thing. I'm excited you asked me."

"If you give me your contact info, I can forward it to my sister Hope. She's really the one in charge."

"Your name is Faith and you have a sister named Hope. Let me guess, do you have another one named Charity?"

"That would be logical, wouldn't it? But my parents never did what was expected. They named our youngest sister Celeste."

"Celeste is the children's librarian in town and she's also an author," Ashley said. "And Hope is an illustrator."

"Oh! Of course! Celeste and Hope Nichols. They wrote 'Sparkle and the Magic Snowball'! The kids at the developmental skills center where I used to work loved that story. They even wrote a song about Sparkle."

Faith smiled. "You'll have to share it with Celeste and Hope. They'll be thrilled."

She and Ella were sending contact information to each other's phones when she felt a subtle ripple in the air and a moment later Chase joined them.

Speaking with the women had begun to push out some of the butterflies inside her but they suddenly returned in full force.

"Sorry I was gone so long. I got cornered by Pete Jeppeson at the coatrack and just barely managed to get away."

"No worries. I've been meeting someone who is about to make my sisters very, very happy. Chase Brannon, this is Ella Baker. She's Curt's daughter and she's a music therapist who has just agreed to help out with the second annual Christmas Ranch holiday show."

Chase gave Ella a warm smile. "That's very kind of you—not to mention extremely brave."

The woman returned his smile and Faith didn't miss the sudden appreciative light in her eyes, along with a slightly regretful look, the sort a woman might wear while shopping when someone else in line at the checkout just ahead of her picks out the exact one-of-a-kind piece of jewelry she would have chosen for herself.

"Brave or crazy," Ella said. "I'm not sure which yet."

"You said it. I didn't," Chase said.

Both of them laughed and as she saw them together, a strange thought lodged in her brain.

The two of them could be perfect for each other.

She didn't want to admit it but Ella Baker seemed on the surface just the sort of woman Chase needed. She had only just met the woman but she trusted her instincts. Ella seemed smart and pretty, funny and kind.

Exactly the sort of woman Chase deserved.

He said he was ready to date again and here was a perfect candidate. Wouldn't a truehearted friend do everything in her power to push the two of them together—at least give Chase the chance to get to know the other woman?

She hated the very idea of it, but she wanted Chase to be happy. "Will you both excuse me for a moment? I just spotted Jenna McRaven and remembered I need to talk to her about a slight change in the menu for the dinner next week."

She aimed a bright smile at them. "You two should dance or something. Go ahead! I won't be long."

She caught a glimpse of Ella's startled features and the beginnings of a thundercloud forming on Chase's but she hurried away before he could respond.

He would thank her later, she told herself, especially if Ella turned out to be absolutely perfect for him.

He only needed to spend a little time with her to realize the lovely young woman who had put her life on hold to help her ailing father was a much better option than a prickly widow who didn't have anything left in her heart to give him.

She found Jenna in the kitchen, up to her eyeballs in appetizers.

This was the absolute worst time to bug her about a catering job, when she was busy at a different one. Faith couldn't bother her with a small change in salad dressing—especially when she was only using this as an excuse to leave Chase alone with Ella Baker. She would call Jenna later and tell her about the change at a better time.

"Hi, Faith! Don't you look beautiful tonight!"

She almost gave an inelegant snort. Jenna's blond curls were piled on her head in an adorable messy bun and her cheeks looked rosy from the heat of the kitchen and probably from the exertion of preparing a meal for so many people, while Faith had split ends and hands desperately in need of a manicure.

"I was just going to say the same to you," she said. "Seriously, you're the only person I know who can be neck-deep in making canapés and still manage to look like a model."

Jenna rolled her eyes as she continued setting out appetizers on the tray. "You're sweet but delusional. Did you need something?"

Faith glanced through the open doorway, where she could see Chase bending down to listen more closely to something Ella was saying. The sight made her stomach hurt—but maybe that was just hunger.

"Not at all. I was just wondering if you need any help back here."

Jenna looked startled at her question but not ungrateful. "That's very sweet but I'm being paid to hang out here in the kitchen. You're not. You should be out there enjoying the party."

"I can hear the music from here, plus helping you out in the kitchen would give me the chance to talk to a dear friend I don't see often enough. Need me to carry out a tray or two?"

Jenna blew out a breath. "I should say no. You're a

guest at the party. I hate to admit it, but I could really use some help for a minute. It's a two-person job but my assistant has the flu so I'm a little frantic here. Carson will be here to help me as soon as he can, but his flight from San Francisco was delayed because of weather so he's running about an hour behind."

Faith found it unbearably sweet that Jenna's billionaire husband—who commuted back and forth between Silicon Valley and Pine Gulch—was ready to help the wife he adored with a catering job. "I can help you until he gets here. No problem."

Jenna lifted her head from her task long enough to frown. "Didn't I see you come in with Chase when I was out replenishing the Parmesan smashed potatoes? I can't let you just ditch him."

She glanced at the door where he was now smiling at something Ella said.

"We drove here together, yes," she answered. "But I'm hoping he'll be dancing with Curt Baker's daughter in a moment."

"Oh. Ella. Jolie just started taking piano lessons from her. She's a delight."

"I think she would be great for Chase so I'm trying to give them a chance to get to know each other. Let nature take its course and all."

Jenna's busy hands paused in her work and she gave Faith a careful look. "You might want to ask Chase his opinion on that idea," she said mildly.

"I don't need to ask him. He's my best friend. I know what he needs probably better than he knows himself."

Jenna opened her mouth to answer, then appeared to think better of it.

She was right, Faith told herself. Chase would thank her later; she was almost certain of it.

## *Chapter Five*

Faith was trying to ditch him.

He knew exactly what she was doing as she moved in and out of the kitchen carrying trays of food for Jenna McRaven's catering company. It wasn't completely unusual for her to help out behind the scenes, but he knew in this case she was just looking for an excuse to avoid him.

He curled his hands into fists, trying to decide if he was more annoyed or hurt. Either way, he still wanted to punch something.

The woman beside him hummed along with the bluegrass version of "Silver Bells." Ella Baker had a pretty voice and kind eyes. He felt like a jerk for ignoring her while he glowered after Faith, even though Ella wasn't the date he had walked in with.

"What were you doing before you came back to Pine Gulch to stay with your father?" he asked.

"I was the music instructor at a residential school for developmentally delayed children in Upstate New York, the same town where you can find the boarding school I attended myself from the age of eight, actually."

Boarding school? What was the story there? He wouldn't have taken Curt Baker as the sort of guy to send his kid to boarding school to be raised by someone else most of the year. He couldn't imagine it—it was hard enough packing Addie off to live with her mother half the time.

"Sounds like you were doing good work."

"I found it very rewarding. Some of my students have made remarkable progress. Music can be a comfort and a joy, as well as open doors to language and auditory processing skills I wouldn't have imagined before I started in this field."

"That sounds interesting."

She made a face. "To me, anyway. Sorry. I tend to get a little passionate when I talk about my job."

"I admire that in a person."

"It's not all I do, I promise. I did play piano and I sing in a jazz trio on the weekends."

"That's great! Maybe you ought to perform at the holiday show yourself."

She made a face. "I probably would be a little out of place, since it sounds like this is mostly a show featuring children. I'm happy enough behind the scenes."

The band changed to a slower song, a wistful holiday tune about regret and lost loves.

"Oh, I love this song," she exclaimed, swaying a little in time to the music.

What was the etiquette here? He had come to the party with a woman who was doing her best to stay away from him. Meanwhile another one was making it clear she wanted to dance.

He didn't know the social conventions but he figured simple politeness trumped the rules anyway.

"Would you like to dance?" he finally asked. If Faith would rather hide out in the kitchen than spend time in conversation with him, he probably wasn't committing some grave faux pas by asking another woman for a simple dance.

Ella's smile was soft with delight. "I would, actually. Thanks."

How weird was this night turning out? Chase wondered as he led the woman out to the dance floor with about a dozen other couples. He had come to the party hoping to end up with Faith in his arms. Instead, she was currently busy carrying out a pot of soup while he was dancing with a woman he had only just met.

Ella was a good conversationalist. She asked him about his ranch and Pine Gulch and the surroundings. He told her about Addie and the cruise she was going on with her mother and stepfather over the holidays and his plans to have their own Christmas celebration a few days before the twenty-fifth.

He actually enjoyed himself more than he might have expected, though beneath the enjoyment he was aware of a simmering frustration at Faith.

When the song ended, he spotted Ella's father on

the edge of the dance floor speaking with a ranching couple he knew who lived up near Driggs. He led her there, visited with the group for a moment, then made his excuses and headed straight for the kitchen.

He found Faith plating pieces of apple pie. She was talking to Jenna McRaven but her words seemed to stall when she spotted him.

"Are you going to hide out in here all night?"

Her gaze shifted away from his but not before he saw the shadow of nervousness there. "I'm not hiding out," she protested. "I was just giving Jen a hand for a minute. Anyway, you've been busy dancing with Ella Baker."

Only because his real date was as slippery as a newborn calf.

"You've done more than enough," Jenna assured her. "I'm grateful for your help but I'm finally caught up in here. Carson's plane just landed and he's on his way here to help me with the rest of the night. You really need to go out and enjoy the party."

Faith opened her mouth to protest but Jenna gave her a stern look. "I'm serious, sweetie. Go out and enjoy all this delicious food I've been slaving over for a week. Now hand over the apron and back away slowly and nobody will get hurt."

"Fine. If you insist." Faith huffed out a little breath but untied her apron and set it on an empty space on the counter. Chase wasn't about to let her wriggle away again. He hooked his hand in the crook of her elbow and steered her out into the reception hall and over to the buffet line.

They grabbed their food, which all appeared delicious, then Faith scanned the room. "I see a couple of chairs over by Em and Ashley. Why don't we go sit with them?"

He enjoyed hanging out with their neighbors but right now he would rather find a secluded corner and have this out. Barring that, he would rather just go home and get the hell out of this suit and tie.

Nothing was working out as he planned and he felt stupid and shortsighted for thinking it might.

"Sure. Sounds good," he lied.

She led the way and as soon as they were seated, she immediately launched into a long conversation with the other couples.

By the time dinner was over, he was more than ready to throw up his hands and declare the evening a disaster, convinced she was too stubborn to ever consider they could be anything but friends.

Sitting at this table with their neighbors and friends filled him with a deep-seated envy that left him feeling small. They were all long-married yet still obviously enamored with each other, with casual little touches and private smiles that left him feeling more lonely than ever.

The band had begun to move away from strictly playing holiday songs and began a cover of a popular upbeat pop song, adding a bluegrass flair, of course. Ashley Hartford lit up. "Oh! I love this song. Come dance with me, darling."

Though they had four children and had been married for years, Justin gave her the sort of smoldering look Chase guessed women enjoyed, since the man had made millions on the big screen, before he walked away from it all to come to Pine Gulch.

"Let's do it," he said.

"We can't let them show us up," Emery declared to her husband. "I know you hate to dance but will you, just this once?"

Nate Cavazos, former army Special Forces and tough as nails, sighed but obediently rose to follow his petite wife out to the dance floor. Their departure left him alone at the table with Faith, along with an awkward silence.

He gestured to the floor. "Do you want to dance?"

Panic flickered in her eyes and his gut ached. She had been his friend for nearly two decades. They had laughed together, cried together, confided secrets to each other.

Why the hell couldn't she see they were perfect for each other?

"Forget it," he said. "You're not enjoying this. Why don't I just go get Celeste's fabulous coat and we can take off?"

Her lush mouth twisted into a frown. "That's not fair to you."

She looked at the dance floor for a moment, then back at him. "Actually, let's go dance. I would like it very much."

He wanted to call her out for the lie but it seemed stupid to argue. Instead, Chase scraped his chair back, then reached a hand out. She placed her slim, cool, working-rancher hand in his and he led her out to the dance floor.

Just as they reached it, the music shifted to a song

he didn't know, something slow and dreamy, jazzy and soft. He pulled her into his arms—finally!—and they began to move in time to the music.

"This is nice," she murmured, and he took that as encouragement to pull her a little closer. She smelled delicious, that subtle scent he had picked up earlier, and he closed his eyes and tried to burn the moment into his memory.

She stumbled a little and when he glanced down, she was blushing. "Sorry. I'm not very good at this. I never learned to dance, unless you count some of the native dances we did in South America and Papua New Guinea."

"I'd like to see some of those."

She laughed. "I doubt I could remember a single one. Hope probably can. She was always more into them than I was. You're a very good dancer. Why didn't I know that?"

"I guess we haven't had much call to dance together."

His mother had taught him, he remembered, when he was about fourteen or fifteen, before his father's diagnosis and his family fell apart.

His mother had told him he needed to learn so he wouldn't be embarrassed at school dances. Turns out, he hadn't needed the lessons. His father's cancer and the toll the treatment had taken on him had left Chase little time for frivolous things like proms. It was all he could do to keep the ranch running while his mother ran his dad back and forth to the cancer center in Salt Lake City.

Despite the long, difficult fight, his father had lost

the battle. After he died, things had been worse. His mother had completely fallen apart that first year and had slipped into a deep, soul-crushing depression that lasted for a tough four years, until she finally went to visit a sister in Seattle, fell in love with a restaurant owner she met there and moved there permanently.

Sometimes he wondered what might have happened if his father hadn't died, if Chase hadn't been forced to put his own plans for college on the back burner.

If he had been in a better place to pursue Faith first.

If.

It was a word he really hated.

A few more turns around the dance floor and she appeared to relax and seemed to be enjoying the music and the moment. He even made her laugh a few times. The music shifted into another slow dance and she didn't seem in a hurry to stop dancing so he decided to just go with it.

If he had his choice, he would have frozen that moment forever in time, just savoring the scent of her hair and the way her curves brushed against him and the way she fit so perfectly in his arms.

Too quickly, the music ended and she pulled away.

"That was nice," she said. "Thanks."

Dancing with him had been a big step for her, he knew.

"They're about to serve dessert," he said on impulse. "What do you say we grab a couple slices of that apple pie in a couple of to-go boxes and take off somewhere to enjoy it where we can look at Christmas lights?"

"We don't have to leave if you're enjoying yourself."

"I just want to be with you. I really don't care where."

He probably shouldn't have been that blunt. She nibbled on her lip, clearly mulling her options, then smiled.

"Let's go."

She hated being a coward.

Her sister Hope plowed through life, exploring the world as their parents had, experiencing life and collecting friends everywhere she went. Celeste, the youngest, was shy and timid and could be socially awkward. That seemed to have changed significantly since her marriage to Flynn and since her literary career took off, requiring more public appearances and radio interviews. Celeste seemed to be far more comfortable in her own skin these days.

Now Faith was the timid one.

Losing her husband and becoming a widow at thirty-two had changed her in substantial ways. Sometimes she wasn't even sure who she was anymore.

She had never considered herself particularly brave, though she had tried to put on a strong front for Hope and Celeste after their parents died. They had needed her and while she wanted to curl up into herself, she had tried to set an example of courage for her sisters.

After Travis died, she had wanted to do the same. That time, her children had needed her. She had to show them that even in the midst of overwhelming grief they could survive and even thrive.

Right now, that facade of strength seemed about to crumble to dust. In her heart, she was terrified and it seemed to be growing worse. She was so afraid of shaking up the status quo, setting herself up for more pain.

More than that, she was afraid of hurting Chase.

She wouldn't worry about that now. Once they were alone, just the two of them, they could forget all this date nonsense and just be Chase and Faith again, like always.

Jenna McRaven didn't ask questions when they asked if she had any to-go boxes. She pulled out a cardboard container that she loaded with two pieces of caramel-topped apple pie.

A moment later, without giving explanations to anyone, they grabbed Celeste's luxurious coat and hurried outside into the December night.

Her breath puffed out as they made their way to his pickup but she wasn't cold. She wanted to give credit to the fine cashmere wool but in truth she was still overheated from the warm dance floor and her own ridiculous nerves.

"Where should we go for dessert?" he asked. "What do you think about Orchard Park? It offers a nice view of town."

She would rather go back to the Star N and change into jeans and a T-shirt. Barring that, Orchard Park would have to do. "Sounds good," she answered.

He turned on a Christmas station and soft, jazzy music filled the interior of his pickup truck as he drove the short distance from the reception hall to an area of new development in Pine Gulch.

A small subdivision of single-family homes was being built here on land that had once been filled with fruit trees. The streets had names like Apple Blossom Drive, Jubilee Lane and McIntosh Court and only about half the lots had new houses.

Chase pulled above the last row of houses to a clearing at the end of the road, probably where the developer planned to add more houses eventually.

He put the vehicle in Park but left the engine running. Warm air poured out of the vents from the heater, wrapping them in a cozy embrace.

"I'm sorry I didn't think to get a bottle of wine but I should have some water in my emergency stash."

He climbed out and rummaged in a cargo box in the backseat before emerging with a couple of water bottles.

Given the harsh winters in the region, most people she knew kept kits in their vehicles with water bottles, granola bars and foil emergency blankets in case they were stranded in a blizzard.

"Don't forget to replenish your supply," she said when he slid back in the front seat.

"I won't. Nothing worse than being stuck in four-foot-high drifts somewhere with nothing to drink but melted snow."

That had never happened to her, thankfully. She unscrewed the cap and took a drink of the water, which was remarkably cold and refreshing, then handed him the to-go carton of pie Jenna had given them along with the fork her friend had provided.

"I guess it's fitting we should eat an apple pie here," she said.

His teeth gleamed in the darkness as he smiled. "Anything else wouldn't seem as appropriate, would it?"

With the glittery stars above them and the color-ful lights of town below, she took a bite of her pie and nearly swooned from the sheer sensory overload.

"Wow. That's fantastic," she breathed. It was flaky and crusty and buttery, with just the right hint of cara-mel. "Jenna is a master of the simple apple pie. I've got her recipe but I can never make it just like this. I don't know what she does differently from me or Aunt Mary or my sisters but it's so fantastic."

"Even without ice cream."

She laughed. "I was thinking that but didn't want to say it."

It seemed a perfect moment, so much better away from the public social pressure of the party. She took a deep breath and realized she hadn't fully filled her lungs all evening. Stupid nerves.

"I love the view from this area," she said. "Pine Gulch seems so peaceful and quiet."

"I suppose it looks so peaceful because you can't see from up here how old Doris Packer is such a bitter old hag or how Ben Tillman has a habit of shortchang-ing his customers at the tavern or how Wilma Rivera is probably talking trash about her sister-in-law."

He was so right. "It's easy to simply look at the sur-face and think you know a place, isn't it?"

"Right." He sent her a sidelong look. "People are much the same. You have to dig beneath the nice clothes and the polite polish to find the essence of a person."

She knew the essence of Chase Brannon. He was a kind, decent, *good* man who so deserved to be happy.

She sighed and could feel the heat of his gaze.

"That sounded heavy. What's on your mind?"

She had a million things racing through her thoughts and didn't know how to talk to him about any of it. She couldn't tell him that she felt like she stood on the edge of a precipice, toes tingling from the vast, unknown chasm below her, and she just didn't know how much courage she had left inside her to jump.

"I'm feeling bad about taking you away from the party," she lied.

"You didn't take me away. Leaving was my idea, remember?"

He reached up to loosen his tie. Funny how that simple act seemed to help her remember this was Chase, her best friend. She wanted him to be happy, no matter what.

"It was a good idea. Still, if we had stayed, maybe you could have danced with Ella Baker again."

He said nothing but annoyance suddenly seemed to radiate out of him in pointed rays.

"She seems very nice," Faith pressed.

"Yes."

"And she's musical, too."

"Yes."

"Not to mention beautiful, don't you think?"

"She's lovely."

"You should ask her out, since you suddenly want to start dating again."

He made a low sound in the back of his throat, the kind of noise he made when his tractor broke down or one of his ranch hands called in sick too many times.

"Who said I wanted to start dating again?" he said, his voice clipped.

"You did. You're the one who insisted this was a *date-date*. You made a big deal that it wasn't just two friends carpooling to the stockgrowers' party together, remember?"

"That doesn't mean I'm ready to start dating again, at least not in general terms. It only means I'm ready to start dating *you*."

There it was.

Out in the open.

The reality she had been trying so desperately to avoid. He wanted more from her than friendship and she was scared out of her ever-loving mind at the possibility.

The air in the vehicle suddenly seemed charged, crackling with tension. She had to say something but had no idea what.

"I... Chase—"

"Don't. Don't say it."

His voice was low, intense, with an edge to it she rarely heard. She had so hoped they could return to the easy friendship they had always known. Was that gone forever, replaced by this jagged uneasiness?

"Say...what?"

"Whatever the hell you were gearing up for in that tone of voice like you were knocking on the door to tell me you just ran over my favorite dog."

"What do you want me to say?" she whispered.

"I sure as hell don't want you trying to set me up with another woman when you're the only one I want."

She stared at him, the heat in his voice rippling down

her spine. She swallowed hard, not knowing what to say as awareness seemed to spread out to her fingertips, her shoulder blades, the muscles of her thighs.

He was so gorgeous and she couldn't help wondering what it would be like to taste that mouth that was only a few feet away.

He gazed down at her for a long, charged moment, then with a muffled curse, he leaned forward on the bench seat and lowered his mouth to hers.

Given the heat of his voice and the hunger she thought she glimpsed in his eyes, she might have expected the kiss to be intense, fierce.

She might have been able to resist that.

Instead, it was much, much worse.

It was soft and unbearably sweet, with a tenderness that completely overwhelmed her. His mouth tasted of caramel and apples and the wine he'd had at dinner—delectable and enticing—and she was astonished by the urge she had to throw her arms around him and never let go.

## Chapter Six

For nearly fifteen years, he had been trying *not* to imagine this moment.

When she was married to one of his closest friends, he had no idea she tasted of apples and cinnamon, that she smelled like oranges and vanilla sprinkled across a meadow of wildflowers.

He hadn't wanted to know she made tiny little sounds of arousal, little breathy sighs he wanted to capture inside his mouth and hold there forever.

It was easier *not* knowing those things. He could see that now.

He had hugged her many times and already knew how perfectly she fit against him. Sometimes when they would come back from traveling out of town together— Idaho Falls for the livestock auction or points farther away to pick up ranch equipment or parts—she would fall asleep, lulled by the motion of the vehicle and the rare chance to sit in one place for longer than five minutes.

He loved those times. Invariably, she would end up curled against him, her head on his shoulder. It would always take every ounce of strength he possessed not to pull her close, tuck her against him and drive off into the sunset.

He had always tried to remember his place as her friend, her support system.

Aching and wistful, he would spend those drives wishing he could keep driving a little extra or that when they arrived at their destination, he could gently turn her face to his and wake her with a kiss.

It was a damn good thing he hadn't ever risked something so stupid. If he had, he would never have been able to let her go.

He had her now, though, and he wasn't about to let this moment go to waste. She needed to see that she was still a lovely, sensual woman who couldn't spend the rest of her life hidden away at the Star N, afraid to let anybody else inside.

If he couldn't talk her into giving him a chance, perhaps he could seduce her into it.

It wasn't the most honorable thought he'd ever had, but right now, with her mouth warm and open against his and her silky hair under his fingertips, he didn't care.

He deepened the kiss and she froze for a second, and then her lips parted and she welcomed him inside, her tongue tangling with his and her hands clutching his shirt.

She might never be able to love him as he wanted but at least she should know she was a beautiful, desirable woman who had an entire life ahead of her.

He wasn't sure how long they spent wrapped around each other. What guy could possibly pay attention to insignificant little details like that when the woman he loved was kissing him with abandon?

He only knew he had never been so grateful for his decision to get a bench seat in his pickup instead of two buckets. Without a console in the way, she was nearly in his lap, exactly where he wanted her...

This was the dumbest thing he had ever done.

Even as he tried to lose himself in the kiss, the thought seemed to slither across his mind like a rattle-snake across his boot.

He was only setting himself up for more heartache. He should have thought this through, looked ahead past the moment and what he wanted right now.

How could he ever go back to being friends with her, trying like hell to be respectful of the subtle distance she so carefully maintained between them? He couldn't scrub these moments from his mind. Every time he looked at her now, he would remember this cold, star-filled night with the glittering holiday lights of Pine Gulch spread out below them and her warm, delicious mouth tangling with his.

Some small but powerful instinct for self-preservation clamored at him that maybe he better stop this while he still could, before all these years of pent-up desire burst through his control like irrigation water through a busted wheel line. He couldn't completely lose his head here.

He drew in a sharp breath and eased away from her. Her features were a pale blur in the moonlight but her lips were swollen from his kiss, her eyes half-closed. Her hair was tousled from his hands and she looked completely luscious.

He nearly groaned aloud at the effort it took to slide away from her when his entire body was yelling at him to pull her closer.

She opened her eyes and gazed at him, pupils dilated and her ragged breathing just about the most erotic sound he'd ever heard.

He saw the instant awareness returned to her eyes. They widened with shock and something else, then color soaked her cheeks.

She untangled her hands from around his neck and eased away from him.

"It's been a long time since I made out with a pretty girl in a pickup truck," he said into the suddenly heavy silence. "I forgot how awkward it could be."

She swallowed hard. "Right," she said slowly. "It's the pickup truck making things awkward."

They both knew it was much more than that. It was the years of history between them and the weight of a friendship that was important to both of them.

"I so wish you hadn't done that," she said in a small voice.

Her words carved out another little slice of his heart.

"Which? Kissed you? Or stopped?"

She shifted farther away from him and turned her face to look out at the town below them.

Instead of answering him directly, she offered up what seemed to him like a completely random change of topic.

"Do you remember the first time we met?"

Of course he remembered. Most guys remembered the days that left them feeling as if they had been run over by a tractor.

"Yes. You and your sisters had only been here with Mary and Claude a day or two."

"It was February 18, a week after our mother's funeral. We had been in Idaho exactly forty-eight hours."

She remembered it so exactly? He wasn't sure what to think about that. He only remembered that he had been sent by his mother to drop off a meal for "Mary's poor nieces."

The whole community knew what had happened to her and her sisters—that their parents had been providing medical care in a poor jungle town in Colombia when the entire family had been kidnapped by rebels looking for a healthy ransom.

After all these years, he still didn't know everything that had happened to her in that rebel camp. She didn't talk about it and he didn't ask. He did know her father had been shot and killed by rebels during a daring rescue mission orchestrated by US Navy SEALs, including a very young Rafe Santiago, now Hope's husband.

He didn't know much more now than he had that first time he met her. When the news broke a few months earlier and her family returned to the US, it had been big news in town. How could it be otherwise, given that her father had grown up in Pine Gulch and everyone knew the family's connection to Claude and Mary?

Unfortunately, the family's tragedy hadn't ended with her father's death. After their rescue, her mother had been diagnosed with an aggressive cancer that might have been treatable if she hadn't been living in primitive conditions for years—and if she hadn't spent the last month as a hostage in a rebel camp.

That had been Chase's mother's opinion, anyway. She had been on her way out of town to his own father's cancer treatment but had told him to drop off a chicken rice casserole and a plate of brownies to the Nichols family.

He remembered being frustrated at the order. Why couldn't she have dropped it off on her way out of town? Didn't he have enough to do on the ranch, since he was basically running things single-handedly?

Claude had answered the door, with the phone held to his ear, and told him Mary was in the kitchen and to go on back. He had complied, not knowing the next few moments would change his life.

He vividly remembered that moment when he had seen Faith standing at the sink with Mary, peeling potatoes.

She had been slim and pretty and fragile, with huge green eyes, that sweet, soft mouth and short, choppy blond hair—which she later told him she had cut herself with a butter knife sharpened on a brick, because of lice in the rebel camp.

He also suspected it had been an effort to avoid unwanted attention from the rebels, though she had never told him that. He couldn't imagine they couldn't see past her choppy hair to the rare beauty beneath.

Yeah, a guy tended to remember the moment he lost his heart.

"I gave you a ride into town," he said now. "Mary needed a gallon of milk or something."

"That's what she said, anyway," Faith said, her mouth tilted up a little. "I think she only wanted me to get out of the house and have a look at our new community and also give me a chance to talk to someone around my own age."

Not *that* close in age. He had been eighteen and had felt a million years older.

She had been so serious, he remembered, her eyes solemn and watchful and filled with a pain that had touched his heart.

"Whatever the reason, I was happy to help out."

"Everyone else treated us like we were going to crack apart at any moment. You were simply kind. You weren't overly solicitous and you didn't treat me like I had some kind of contagious disease."

She turned to face him, still smiling softly at the memories. "That was the best afternoon I'd had in *forever*. You told me jokes and you showed me the bus stop and the high school and the places where the kids in Pine Gulch liked to hang out. At the grocery store, you introduced me to everyone we met and made sure cranky Mr. Gibbons didn't cheat me, since I didn't have a lot of experience with American money."

She had been an instant object of attention everywhere they went, partly because she was new to town and partly because she looked so exotic, with a half-dozen woven bracelets on each wrist, the choppy hair, her wide, interested eyes.

"A few days later, you came back and said you were heading into town and asked if Aunt Mary needed you to come with me to pick anything else up."

That had basically been a transparent ploy to spend more time with her, which everyone else had figured out but Faith.

"That meant so much to me," she said. "Your own father was dying but that didn't stop you from reaching out and trying to help me acclimatize. I've never forgotten how kind you were to me."

Was it truly kindness, when he was the one who had benefited most? "It couldn't have been easy to find yourself settled in a small Idaho town, after spending most of your childhood wandering around the world."

"It was easier for me than it was for Hope and Celeste, I think. All I ever wanted was to stay in one place for a while, to have the chance to make friends finally. Friends like you."

She gave him a long, steady look. "You are my oldest and dearest friend, Chase. Our friendship is one of the most important things in my life."

He wanted to squeeze her hand, to tell her he agreed with her sentiments completely, but he didn't dare touch her again right now.

"Ditto," he said gruffly.

She drew in a breath that seemed to hitch a little. She looked out the windshield, where a few clouds had

begun to gather, spitting out stray snowflakes that spi-
raled down and caught the light of the stars.

"That's why I have to ask you not to kiss me again."

## *Chapter Seven*

Though she didn't raise her voice, her hard-edged words seemed to echo through his pickup truck.

*I have to ask you not to kiss me again.*

She meant what she said. He knew that tone of voice. It was the same one she used with the kids when meting out punishment for behavioral infractions or with cattle buyers when they tried to negotiate and offered a price below market value.

Her mind was made up and she wouldn't be swayed by anything he had to say.

Tension gripped his shoulders and he didn't know what the hell to say.

"That's blunt enough, I guess," he finally answered. "Funny, but you seemed to be into it at the moment. I guess I misread the signs."

Her mouth tightened. "It's a strange night. Neither of us is acting like ourselves. Can we just…leave it at that?"

That was the last thing he wanted to do. He wanted to kiss her again until she couldn't think straight.

He hadn't misread *any* signs and they both knew it. After that first moment of shock, she returned the kiss with an enthusiasm and eagerness that had left him stunned and hungry.

"Can you just take me home?" she asked in a low voice.

"If that's what you want," he said.

"It is," she answered tersely.

A few moments ago she had wanted *him*.

She was attracted to him. Lately he had been almost sure of it but some part of him had worried his own feelings for her were clouding his judgment. That kiss and her response told him the sexual spark hadn't been one-sided.

Nice to know he was right about that, at least.

She was attracted to him but she didn't want to be. How did a guy work past that conundrum?

The task suddenly seemed insurmountable.

He put the pickup in gear and focused on driving instead of on the growing realization that she might never be willing to accept him as anything more than her oldest and dearest friend.

Maybe, just maybe, it was time he accepted that and moved on with his life.

Though his features remained set and hard as he drove her back to the Star N, Chase carried on a casual conversation with her about the new horse, about a bit of gossip he heard about cattle futures at the stockgrowers' party, about Addie's Christmas presents that still needed to be wrapped.

Under other circumstances, she might have been quite proud of her halfway intelligent responses—especially when she really wanted to collapse into a boneless, quivering heap on the truck seat.

She couldn't stop remembering that kiss—the heat and the magic and the wild intensity of it.

Her heartbeat still seemed unnaturally loud in her ears and she hadn't quite managed to catch her breath, though she could almost manage to string two thoughts together now.

She felt very much like a tiny island in the middle of a vast arctic river just beginning the spring thaw, with chunks of ice and fast-flowing water buffeting against it in equal parts, bringing life back to the frozen landscape.

She didn't *want* to come to life again. She wanted that river of need to stay submerged under a hard layer of impenetrable ice forever.

Knowing that hollow ache was still there, that her sexuality hadn't shriveled up and died with Travis, completely terrified her.

She was a little angry about it, too, if she were honest. Why couldn't she just resume the state of affairs of the last thirty months, that sense of suspended animation?

This was *Chase*. Her best friend. The man she relied on for a hundred different things. How could she possibly laugh and joke with him like always when she would now be remembering just how his mouth had slid across hers, the glide of his tongue, the heat of his muscles against her chest.

She didn't want that river of need to come to churning, seething life again.

Yes, her world had been cold and sterile since Travis died, but it was *safe*.

She felt like she was suffocating suddenly, as if that wild flare of heat between them had consumed all the oxygen.

She rolled her window down a crack and closed her eyes at the welcome blast of cold air.

"Too warm?" he asked.

Oh, yes. He didn't know the half of it. "A little," she answered in a grave understatement.

He turned the fan down on the heating system just as her phone buzzed. She pulled it from the small beaded handbag Celeste had offered for the occasion.

It was a text from her sister: Girls are asleep. Don't rush home. Have fun.

She glanced at the message, then slid her phone back into the totally impractical bag.

"Problem?" he asked.

"Not really. I think Celeste was just checking in. She said the girls are asleep."

"I hope Addie was good."

"She's never any trouble. Really, we love having her around. She always seems to set a good example for my kids."

"Even Barrett?"

She relaxed a little. Talking about their children was much easier than discussing everything else.

"He can be such a rascal when Addie's there. I don't get it. He teases both of them mercilessly. I try to tell him to cut it out but the truth is I think he has a little crush on her."

"Older women. They're nothing but trouble. I had the worst crush on Maggie Cruz but she never paid me the slightest bit of attention. Why would she? I was in fifth grade and she was in eighth and we were on totally different planets."

The only crush she could remember having was the son of the butcher in the last village where they'd lived in Colombia. He had dark, soulful eyes and curly dark hair and always gave her all the best cuts when she went to the market for her family.

That seemed another lifetime ago. She couldn't even remember being that girl who once smiled at a cute boy.

By the time Chase pulled up to the Star N a few moments later, her hormones had almost stopped zinging around.

He put the truck in Park and opened his door.

"Since Addie's asleep, you don't have to come in," she said quickly, before he could climb out. "You don't really have to walk me to the door like this was a real date."

Why did she have to say that? The words seemed to slip out from nowhere and she wanted to wince. She didn't need to remind him of the awkwardness of the evening.

He said nothing, though she didn't miss the way his

mouth tightened and his eyes cooled a fraction before he completely ignored what she said and climbed out anyway.

Everything between them had changed and it made her chest ache with regret.

"Thanks, Chase," she said as they walked side by side through the cold night. "I had a really great time."

"You don't have to lie. It was a disaster from start to finish."

The grim note in his voice made her sad all over again. She sighed. "None of that was your fault. Only mine."

"The old, *it's not you, it's me* line?" he asked as they reached the door. "Really, Faith? You can't be more original than that?"

"It *is* me," she whispered, knowing he deserved the truth no matter how painful. "I'm such a coward and I always have been."

He made a low sound of disbelief. "A coward. You."

"I am!"

"This is the same woman who woke up the day after her husband's funeral, put on her boots and went to work—and who hasn't stopped since?"

"What choice did I have? The ranch was our livelihood. Someone had to run it."

"Right. Just like somebody jumped into a river to save a villager in Guatemala while everybody else was standing on the shore wringing their hands."

She stared at him. "How did you... Where did you hear that?"

"Hope told me once. I think it was after Travis died.

She also told me how you took more than one beating while you were all being held hostage because you stepped up to take responsibility for something she or Celeste had done."

She was the oldest. It had been her job to protect her sisters. What else could she do especially since it was her fault they had all been taken hostage to begin with?

She had told that cute boy she had a crush on the day they were supposed to go to Bogota so her mother could see a doctor and that they would probably be leaving for good in a few weeks.

She had hoped maybe he might want to write to her. Instead, he must have told the psychotic rebel leader their plans. The next time she saw that boy, he had been proudly wearing ragged army fatigues and carrying a Russian-made submachine gun.

"You're not a coward, Faith," Chase said now. "No matter how much you might try to convince yourself of that."

A stray snowflake landed on her cheek and she brushed it away. "You are my best friend, Chase. I'm so afraid of destroying that friendship, like I've screwed up everything else."

He gave her a careful look that made her wish she hadn't said anything, had just told him good-night and slipped into the house.

"Can we... More than anything, I would like to go back to the way things were a few weeks ago. Without all this...awkwardness. When we were just Faith and Chase."

He raised an eyebrow. "You really think we can do that, after that kiss?"

She shivered a little, from more than simply the cold night. "I would like to try. Please, Chase."

"How do two people take a step backward? Something is always lost."

"Can't we at least give it a shot? At least until after the holidays?"

She hoped he couldn't hear the begging tone of her voice that seemed so loud to her.

"I won't wait forever, Faith."

"I know," she whispered.

"Fine. We can talk again after the New Year."

Her relief was so fierce that she wanted to weep. At least she would have his friendship through the holidays. Maybe in a few more weeks, she would be able to find the courage to face a future without his constant presence.

"Thank you. That's the best gift anyone could give me this year."

She reached up to give him a casual kiss on the cheek, the kind she had given him dozens of times before. At the last minute, he turned his head, surprise in his eyes, and her kiss landed on the corner of his mouth.

Instantly, the mood shifted between them and once more she was aware of the heat of him and the coiled muscles and the ache deep within her for him and only him.

He kissed her fully, his mouth a warm, delicious refuge against the cold night. His scent surrounded her—leather and pine and sexy, masculine cowboy—and she desperately wanted to lean into his strength and surrender to the delicious heat that stirred instantly to life again.

Too soon, he stepped away.

"Good night," he said, his eyes dark in the glow from the porch light. He opened the door for her and waited until she managed to force her wobbly knees to carry her inside, then he turned around and walked to his pickup truck.

She really wanted nothing more than to shrug out of Celeste's luxurious coat, kick off her high heels, slip away to her room and climb into bed for the next week or two.

Unfortunately, a welcoming party waited for her inside. Celeste, Flynn and Aunt Mary were at the table with mugs of hot chocolate steaming into the air and what looked like a fierce game of Scrabble scattered around the table—which hardly seemed a fair battle since Celeste was a librarian and an author with a freaky-vast vocabulary.

All three looked up when she walked into the kitchen.

"Chase didn't come in?" Mary asked, clear disappointment on her wrinkled face.

Sometimes Faith thought her great-aunt had a little crush on Chase herself. What other reason did she have for always inviting him over?

"No," she said abruptly.

How on earth was she going to face him, again, now that they had kissed twice?

"How was your date?" Celeste asked. Though the question was casual enough, her sister gave her a searching look and she suddenly wanted desperately to confide in her.

She couldn't do it, at least not with Flynn and Mary listening in. "Fine," she answered.

"Only fine?" Mary asked, clearly surprised.

"Fun," she amended quickly. "Dinner was delicious, of course, and we danced a bit."

"Chase is a great dancer," Mary said, her eyes lighting up. "I could have danced with him all night at Celeste's wedding, except Agatha Lindley kept trying to cut in. I don't think he wanted to dance with her at all but he was just too nice."

"She was there tonight, though she didn't cut in. Unless she tried it when he was busy dancing with Ella Baker."

"Ella Baker?" Celeste frowned. "I don't think I know her."

"She's Curt Baker's daughter. She's moved to Pine Gulch to look after her father."

"The girls at the salon were talking about her when I went for my color this week," Mary said. "She teaches music or something, doesn't she?"

With a jolt, Faith suddenly remembered her conversation with the woman at the beginning of the party, which seemed like a dozen lifetimes ago. "Oh! I have news. Big news! I can't believe I almost forgot."

"You probably had other things on your mind," Flynn murmured, his voice so dry that she shot him a quick look.

Did her lips look as swollen as they felt, tight and achy and full? She really hoped not.

"You owe me so big," she said. "I begged Ella Baker to help out with the Christmas program. I told her my sisters were desperate and she totally agreed to do it!"

Celeste's eyes widened. "Are you kidding? What's wrong with the woman?"

"Nothing. She was very gracious about it and even said it sounded like fun."

"Right. Fun," Celeste said with a shake of her head.

"You had fun, don't deny it," Mary said. "Look how it ended up for you. Married to a hot contractor, tool belt and all."

"Thanks, my dear." Flynn gave a slow grin and picked up Mary's hand and kissed the back of it in a totally un-Flynn-like gesture that made Celeste laugh and Mary blush and pull her hand away.

"That was a definite side benefit," Celeste murmured, and Flynn gave her a private smile that made the temperature in the room shoot up a dozen degrees or so.

"Well, I'm afraid we don't exactly have more hot contractors to go around for Ella Baker," Faith said. "Though I do think she would be absolutely perfect for Chase. I told him so, but for some reason, he didn't seem to want to hear it."

All three of them stared at Faith as if she had just unleashed a rabid squirrel in the kitchen.

"You told Chase you think this Ella Baker would be perfect for him," Celeste repeated, with such disbelief in her voice that Faith squirmed.

"Yes. She seems like a lovely person," she said, more than a little defensive.

"I'm sure she is," Celeste said. "That doesn't mean

you should have tried to set Chase up with her while the two of you were out together on a date. I'll admit I didn't have a lot of experience before I met Flynn but even I know most guys in general probably wouldn't appreciate that kind of thing. Chase in particular probably didn't want to hear you suggest other women you think he ought to date."

Why Chase in particular? She frowned, though she was aware she had botched the entire evening from the get-go. How was she possibly going to fix things between them?

"We're friends," she retorted. "That's the kind of things friends do for each other, pick out potential dating prospects."

None of them seemed particularly convinced and she was too exhausted to press the point. It was none of their business anyway.

She pulled off Celeste's coat and hung it over one of the empty chairs and also pulled all her personal things out of the little evening bag.

"Thanks for letting me use your coat and bag."

"You're welcome. Anytime."

Right. She wasn't going to another stockgrowers' party. *Ever.*

"I'm going to go change into something comfortable."

"I'll come help you with the zipper. That one sticks, if I remember correctly."

"I don't need help," she said.

"That, my dear, is a matter of opinion."

Celeste rose and followed her up the stairs. As she

helped Faith out of the dress, her sister talked of the children and what they had done that evening and about the latest controversy at the library.

Beneath the light conversation, she sensed Celeste had something more to say. She wasn't sure she wanted to hear it but she couldn't stand the charged subtext either.

After she changed into her favorite comfy pajamas, she sat on the edge of her bed and finally braced herself. "Okay. Out with it."

Celeste deliberately avoided her gaze, confirming Faith's suspicions. "Out with what?" she asked, her tone vague.

"Whatever is lurking there on your tongue, dying to spill out. I can tell you have something to say. You might as well get it over with, for both our sakes. What did I do wrong?"

After a pause, Celeste sat down next to her on the bed.

"I'm trying to figure out if you're being deliberately obtuse or if you honestly don't know—all while I'm debating whether it's any of my business anyway."

"Remember what mom used to say? Better to keep your nose in a book than in someone else's business. Most of your life, you've had a pretty good track record in that department. Don't ruin it now."

Celeste sighed. "Fine. Deliberately obtuse it is, then."

She pulled her favorite sweatshirt over her head. This was more like it, in her favorite soft pajama bottoms and a comfortable hoodie. She felt much more at ease dressed like this than she ever would in the fancy clothes she had been wearing all evening.

"I don't know about *deliberate* but I'll admit I must be obtuse, since I have no idea what you're trying to dance around here."

"Really? No idea?"

The skepticism in her sister's voice burned. "None. What did I do wrong? I was careful with your coat, I promise."

"For heaven's sake, this isn't about the stupid coat."

"I'm not in the mood to play twenty questions with you. If you don't want to tell me, don't."

Celeste's mouth tightened. "Fine. I'll come out and say it, then. Can you honestly tell me you have no idea Chase is in love with you?"

At her sister's blunt words, all the blood seemed to rush away from her brain and she was very glad she was sitting down. Her skin felt hot for an instant and then icy, icy cold.

"Shut up. He is not."

Celeste made a disgusted sound. "Of course he is, Faith! Open your eyes! He's been in love with you *forever*. You had to have known!"

Whatever might be left of the apple pie and the small amount she had eaten at dinner seemed to congeal into a hard, greasy lump in her stomach.

She didn't know whether to laugh at the ridiculous joke that wasn't really funny at all or to tell her sister she was absolutely insane to make such an outrageous accusation. Underneath both those reactions was a tangled surge of emotion and the sudden burn of tears.

"He's not. He *can't* be," she whispered.

It couldn't be true. Could it?

Celeste squeezed her fingers gently, looking as if she regretted saying anything. "Use your head, honey. He's a good neighbor, yes, and a true friend. But can you really not see that his concern for you goes way beyond simple friendship?"

Chase was always there, a true and loyal friend. The one constant, unshakable force in her world.

"I don't want him to be." Her chest felt tight now and she could feel one of those tears slip free. "What am I going to do?"

Celeste squeezed her fingers. "You could try being honest with yourself and admit that you have feelings for him, too."

"As a friend. That's all," she insisted.

Celeste's eyes were full of compassion and exasperation in equal measures. "I love you dearly, Faith. You know I do. You've been my second mother since the day I was born, and from the time I was twelve years old you helped Aunt Mary and Uncle Claude raise me. You're kind and loving, a fantastic mom to Barrett and Lou, a ferociously hard worker. You've taught me so much about what it is to be a good person."

She tugged her hand away, sensing her sister had plenty more to say, and steeled herself to hear the rest.

"But?"

Celeste huffed out a breath. "But when it comes to Chase Brannon, you are being completely stupid and, as much as I hate to say it, more than a little cruel."

"That's a harsh word."

"The man is in love with you and when you sit there pretending you didn't know, you are lying to me, yourself and especially to Chase."

"He has never *once* said anything." She still couldn't make herself believe it.

"The last two years, he has shown you in a thousand different ways. You think he comes over three or four times a week to help Barrett with his homework because he loves fourth grade arithmetic? Can anyone really be naive enough to think he adores cleaning out the rain gutters in the spring and autumn because it's his favorite outdoor activity? Does he check the knock in your pickup's engine or help you figure out the ranch accounts or take a look at any sick cattle you might have because he wants to? No! He does all of those things because of *you*."

Faith could come up with a hundred other things he did for her or for the kids or Aunt Mary. That didn't necessary mean he was in *love* with her, only that he was a good, caring man trying to step up and help them after Travis's death.

The nausea inside her now had an element of panic. Had she been ignoring the truth all this time because she simply hadn't wanted to see it? What kind of horrible person was she? It made her feel like the worst kind of user.

"He's my best friend," she whispered. "What would I do without him?"

"I'm afraid you might have to figure that out sooner than you'd like, especially if you can't admit that you might have feelings for him, too."

With that, her sister rose, gave her a quick hug. "We all loved Travis. He was like the big brother I never had. He was a great guy and a good father. But he's gone, honey. You're not. I'll give you the benefit of the doubt and accept that maybe you didn't want to see that Chase is in love with you so you have avoided facing the truth. But now that you know, what are you going to do about it?"

Her sister slipped from the room before she could come up with a response—which was probably a good thing since Faith had no idea how to answer her.

## *Chapter Eight*

"Why couldn't Lou come with us to take me home?" Addie asked Faith as they pulled out of the Star N driveway to head toward Chase's place.

Faith tried to smile but it ended in a yawn. She was completely wrung out after a fragmented, tortured night spent mostly staring up at her ceiling, reliving the evening—those kisses!—and her conversation with Celeste and wondering what she should do.

She must have slept for a few hours, on and off. When she awoke at her five-thirty alarm, all she wanted to do was pull the covers over her head, curl up and block out the world for a week or two.

Faith blinked away the yawn and tried to smile at Chase's daughter again. "She had a few chores to do this morning and I decided it was better for her to finish them as soon as she could. Sorry about that."

Addie gave her a sudden grin. "Oh. I thought it was maybe because you didn't want her to see her Christmas present in the pasture."

She winced. She should have known Addie would figure it out. The girl was too smart for her own britches. She only hoped she could also keep a secret. "How did you know about that?"

"My dad didn't tell me, in case you're wondering. It wasn't that hard to figure it out, though, especially since Lou hasn't stopped talking about the new barrel racing horse she wants. It seemed like too much of a coincidence when I saw a new horse suddenly had shown up in my dad's pasture."

Faith didn't see any point in dissembling. Christmas was only a few weeks away and the secret would be out anyway. "It wasn't a coincidence," she confirmed. "Your dad helped me pick her out and offered to keep her at Brannon Ridge until after Christmas, when we take her to the Dalton ranch to be trained."

"Louisa is going to be so excited!"

"I think so." Her daughter was a smart, kind, *good* girl. Louisa worked hard in school, did her chores when asked and was generally kind to her brother. She had channeled her grief over losing her father at such a young age into a passion for horse riding and Faith wanted to encourage that.

"I won't tell. I promise," Addie said.

"Thank you, honey."

Addie was a good girl, as well. Some children of divorce became troubled and angry—sometimes even manipulative and sly, pitting one parent against the other for their own gain as they tried to navigate the difficult waters of living in two separate households. Addie was the sweetest girl—which seemed a minor miracle, considering her situation.

"Maybe once she's trained, Lou might let me ride her once in a while," the girl said.

Faith didn't miss the wistful note in Addie's voice. "You know, if you want a horse of your own, you could probably talk your dad into it."

Quite frankly, Faith was surprised Chase hadn't already bought a horse for his daughter.

"I know. Dad has offered to get me one since I was like five. It would be nice, but it doesn't seem very fair to have a horse of my own when I could only see it and ride it once or twice a month. My dad would have to take care of it the rest of the time without me."

"I'm sure he wouldn't mind. He already has Tor. It wouldn't be any trouble at all for him to take care of two horses instead of only one."

"Maybe if I lived here all the time," Addie said in a matter-of-fact tone. "It's hard enough, only seeing my dad a few times a month. I hate when I have to go back to Boise. It would be even harder if I had to leave a horse I loved, too."

Faith swallowed around the sudden lump in her throat. The girl's sad wisdom just about broke her heart. "I can understand that. But you do usually spend summers on the ranch," she pointed out. "That's the best time for riding horses anyway."

"I guess." Addie didn't seem convinced. "I just wish I could stay here longer. Maybe come for the whole school year sometime, even if I wouldn't be in the same grade with Louisa."

"Do you think you might come here to go to school at some point?"

"I wish," she said with a sigh. "My mom always says she would miss me too much. I guess she thinks it's okay for Dad to miss me the rest of the time, when I'm with her."

If she hadn't been driving, Faith would have hugged her hard at the forlorn note in her voice. Poor girl, torn between two parents who loved and wanted her. It was an impossible situation for all of them.

She and Addie talked about the girl's upcoming cruise over the holidays with her mother until they arrived at Chase's ranch. When she pulled up to the ranch, she spotted him throwing a bale of hay into the back of his pickup truck like it weighed no more than a basketball.

She shivered, remembering the heat of his mouth on hers, the solid strength of those muscles against her.

On the heels of that thought came the far more disconcerting one born out of her conversation with Celeste.

*The man is in love with you and when you sit there pretending you didn't know, you are lying to me, yourself and especially to Chase.*

Butterflies jumped around in her stomach and she realized her fingers on the steering wheel were trembling.

Oh. This would never do. This was *Chase*, her best

friend. She *couldn't* let things get funky between them. That was exactly what she worried about most.

Celeste had to be wrong. Faith couldn't accept any other possibility.

The moment she turned off the vehicle, Addie opened the door and raced to hug her dad.

Could she just take off now? Faith wondered. She was half-serious, until she remembered Addie's things were still in the back of the pickup truck.

In an effort to push away all the weirdness, she drew in a couple of cleansing breaths. It didn't work as well as she hoped but the extra oxygen made her realize she had probably been taking nervous, shallow breaths all morning, knowing she was going to have to face him again.

She pulled Addie's sleeping bag out from behind the seat and pasted on a casual smile, knowing even as she did it that he would be able to spot it instantly as fake.

When she turned around, she found him and Addie just a few feet away from her. His eyes were shaded by his black Stetson and she couldn't read the expression there but his features were still, his mouth unsmiling.

"Looks like we caught you going somewhere," she said.

"Just down to the horse pasture to check on, uh, things there."

If she hadn't been fighting against the weight of this terrible awkwardness, she might have managed a genuine smile at his attempt be vague.

"You don't need to use code. Your daughter is too smart for either of us."

"You don't have to tell me that." He smiled down at

Addie and something seemed to unfurl inside Faith's chest. He was an excellent father—and not only to his daughter.

Since Travis died, he had become the de facto father figure for Louisa and Barrett. Oh, Rafe and Flynn did an admirable job as uncles and showed her children how good, decent men took care of their families. But Louisa and Barrett turned to Chase for guidance most. They saw him nearly every day. He was the one Louisa had invited when her class at school had a father-daughter dance and that Barrett had taken along to the Doughnuts with Dad reading hour at school.

They loved him—and he loved them in return. That had nothing to do with any of the nonsense Celeste had talked about the night before.

"Did you have fun last night?" Chase asked Addie now.

"Tons," she declared. "We popped popcorn and watched movies and played games. I beat everybody at UNO like three times in a row and Barrett said I was cheating only I wasn't. And then we all opened our sleeping bags under the Christmas tree and put on another movie and I fell asleep. This morning we had hot chocolate with marshmallows and pancakes shaped like snowmen. It was awesome."

"I'm so glad. Here, I can take that stuff."

He reached to grab the sleeping bag and backpack from Faith. As he did, his hand brushed her chest. It was a touch that barely connected through the multiple layers she wore—coat, a fleece pullover and her silk long underwear—but she could hardly hold back a shiver anyway.

"I'll just take it all into the house now," Addie said. "Thanks for the ride, Faith."

"You're very welcome," she said.

After she strapped the bag over her shoulder and Chase handed her the sleeping bag, she waved at Faith and skipped into the house, humming a Christmas carol.

*What a sweet girl*, Faith thought again. She didn't let her somewhat chaotic circumstances impact her enjoyment of the world around her. Faith could learn a great deal from the girl's example.

"I'll add my thanks to you for bringing her home," Chase said. "I appreciate it, though I could have driven over to get her."

"I really didn't mind. I've got to run into Pine Gulch for a few things anyway. Can I bring you back anything from the grocery store?"

They did this sort of thing all the time. He would call her on his way to the feed store and ask if she needed anything. She would bring back a part from the implement store in Idaho Falls if she had to go for any reason.

She really hoped the easy, casual give-and-take didn't change now that everything seemed so different.

"We could use paper towels, I guess," he said, after a pause. "Oh, and dishwasher detergent and dish soap."

"Sure. I can drop it off on my way home."

"No rush. I'll pick it up next time I come over."

"Sounds good," she answered. At his words, her smile turned more genuine. This seemed much like their normal interactions—and if he was talking about coming to the ranch again, at least he wasn't so upset at her that he was going to penalize the kids by staying away.

"Did you hear Jim Laird messed up his knee?" he asked. "Apparently he slipped on ice and wrenched things and Doc Dalton sent him over to Idaho Falls for surgery yesterday. I wondered why he wasn't at the party last night. I was hoping Mary Beth wasn't in the middle of a relapse or something."

She didn't like hearing when bad things happened to their neighbors. Jim was a sweet older man in his seventies whose wife had multiple sclerosis. They ran a small herd of about fifty head and he often bought alfalfa from her.

"As if he didn't have enough on his plate! What is Mary Beth going to do? She can't possibly do the feedings in the winter by herself."

"Wade Dalton, Justin Hartford and I are going to split the load for a few weeks, until he can get around again."

He was always doing things like that for others in the community.

"I want into the rotation. I can take a turn."

"Not necessary. The three of us have it covered."

She narrowed her gaze. "For six months after Travis died, ranchers up and down the Cold Creek stepped up to help us at the Star N. I'm in a good place now, finally, and want to give back when I can."

The ranch wouldn't have survived without help from her neighbors and friends—especially Chase. She had been completely clueless about running a cattle ranch and would have been lost.

Now that she had stronger footing under her, she wanted to start doing her best to pay it forward.

Chase looked as if he wanted to argue but he must have seen the determination in her expression. After a moment, he gave an exasperated sigh.

"Fine. I'll have Wade give you a call to work out the details."

She smiled. "Thanks. I don't mind the early-morning feedings either."

"I'll let Wade know."

There. That was much more like normal. Celeste had to be wrong. Yes, Chase loved her—just as she loved him. They were dear friends. That was all.

"I better run to the store before the shelves are empty. You know how Saturdays get in town."

"I do."

"So paper towels, dish soap and dish detergent. You can pick up everything tomorrow when you come for dinner," she said.

"That would work."

She felt a little more of the tension trickle away. At least he was still planning to come for dinner.

She loved their Sunday night tradition, when she and her sisters and Aunt Mary always fixed a big family meal and invited any neighbors or friends who would care to join them. Chase invariably made it, unless he was driving Addie back to Boise after a weekend visitation.

"Great. I'll see you tomorrow."

He looked as if he wanted to say something more but she didn't give him the chance. Instead, she jumped into her pickup and pulled away, trying her best not to look at him in the rearview mirror, standing lean-hipped and gorgeous and watching after her.

They had survived their first encounter post-kiss. Yes, it had been tense, but not unbearably so. After this, things between them would become more comfortable each time until they were back to the easy friendship they had always enjoyed.

She cared about him far too much to accept any other alternative.

He stood and watched her drive away, fighting the urge to rub the ache in his chest.

The entire time they talked about groceries and hot chocolate and Jim Laird's bum knee, his damn imagination had been back in a starlit wintry night, steaming up the windows of his pickup truck.

That kiss seemed to be all he could think about. No matter what else he might be trying to focus on, his brain kept going back to those moments when he had held her and she had kissed him back with an enthusiasm he had only dreamed about.

Hot on the heels of those delicious memories, though, came the cold, hard slap of reality.

*I have to ask you not to kiss me again.*

She was so stubborn, fighting her feelings with every bit of her. How was he supposed to win against that?

He pondered his dwindling options as he headed inside to find Addie so she could put on her winter clothes and help him feed the horses.

He found her just finishing a call on her cell phone with a look of resignation.

"Who was that?" he asked, though he was fairly sure he knew the answer. He and Cindy were just about the only ones Addie ever talked to on the phone.

"Mom," she said, confirming his suspicion. "She said Grandma is doing better and Grandpa says he doesn't really need her help anymore. She decided to take me back tomorrow so I can finish the last week of school."

Why didn't she call him first to work out the details?

He was surrounded by frustrating women.

"That's too bad. I know you were looking forward to practicing for the show with Louisa."

Her face fell further. "I forgot about that!" she wailed. "If I don't go to practice, I don't know if I can be in the show."

"I'm sure we can talk to Celeste and Hope and get special permission for you to practice at home. You'll be here next weekend and the first part of next week so you'll be able to be at the last few practices."

"I hope they'll let me. I really, really, *really* wanted to be in the Christmas show."

"We'll work something out," he assured her, hoping he wasn't giving her unrealistic expectations. "Meanwhile, why don't you grab your coat and boots. Since you're so smart and already figured out the new horse is for Lou, do you want to meet her for real so you can tell me what you think?"

"Yes!" she exclaimed.

"You'll have to work hard to keep it a secret."

"I know. I would never ruin the surprise."

With that promise, his daughter raced for the mud-room and her winter gear and Chase leaned a hip against the kitchen island to wait for her and tried not to let his mind wander back to those moments in his pickup that were now permanently imprinted on his brain.

Chase headed up the porch steps of the Star N ranch house with a bag of chips in one hand and a bottle of his own homemade salsa in the other, the same thing he brought along to dinner nearly every Sunday.

The lights of the house were blazing a warm wel-come against the cold and snowy Sunday evening but his instincts were still urging him to forget the whole thing and head back home, where he could glower and stomp around in private.

He was in a sour mood and had been since Cindy showed up three hours earlier than planned to pick up Addie, right as they were on their way out the door to go to their favorite lunch place.

It was always tough saying goodbye to his daugh-ter. This parting seemed especially poignant, probably because Addie so clearly hadn't wanted to go. She had dragged her feet about packing up her things, had asked if they could wait to leave until after she and Chase had lunch, had begged to say goodbye to the horses.

Cindy, annoyed at the delays, had turned sharp-tongued and hard, which in turn made Addie more pouty than normal. Addie had finally gone out to her mother's new SUV with tears in her eyes that broke his heart.

Being a divorced father seriously sucked sometimes.

In his crazier moments, he thought about selling the ranch and moving to Boise to be closer to her, though he didn't know what the hell he would do for a living. Ranching was all he knew, all he had ever known. But he would do whatever it took—work in a shoe factory if he had to—if his daughter needed him.

He wasn't sure that was the answer, though. She loved her time here and seemed to relish ranch life, in a way Cindy never had.

With a sigh, he rang the doorbell, grimly aware that much of his sour mood had roots that had nothing to do with Cindy or Addie.

He had been restless and edgy since the last time he rang this doorbell, when he had shown up at this same ranch to pick up Faith for that disaster of a date two nights earlier.

How many mistakes could one man make in a single evening? Part of him wished he could go back and start the whole stupid week over again and just let his relationship with Faith naturally evolve from friendship to something more.

How long would that take, though? He had a feeling he could have given her five years—ten—and she would still have the same arguments.

Despite all his mistakes, he had to hope he hadn't completely screwed up their friendship for good, that things weren't completely wrecked between them now.

As she had a few nights earlier, Aunt Mary was the one who finally answered the doorbell.

"It's about time," she said, planting hands on her hips. "Faith needs a man in the worst way."

He blinked at that, his imagination suddenly on fire. "O-kay."

Mary looked amused and he guessed she could tell immediately what detour his brain had taken.

"She needs your grilling skills," she informed him.

He told himself that wasn't disappointment coursing through him. "Grilling skills. Ah. You're grilling tonight."

"We *would* be, but Faith is having trouble again with that stupid gas grill. I swear that thing has it out for us."

He gestured behind him to the elements just beyond the porch. "You do know it's starting to snow, right?"

Aunt Mary shrugged. "You hardly notice out there, with the patio heater and that cover Flynn built us for the deck. Steaks sounded like a great idea at the time, better than roast or chicken tonight, but now the grill is being troublesome. Rafe and Hope aren't back yet from visiting Joey's mom, and Flynn had to fly out to California to finish a project there. That leaves Celeste, Faith and me. We could really use somebody with a little more testosterone to figure out what we're doing wrong."

"I'm not an expert on gas grills but I'll see what I can do."

"Thanks, honey."

He followed Mary inside, where they were greeted by delectable smells of roasting potatoes and yeasty rolls. No place on earth smelled better than this old ranch house on Sunday evenings.

"I've got to finish the salad. Go on ahead," Mary said.

He walked through the kitchen to the door that led to the covered deck. Faith didn't see him at first; she was too busy swearing and fiddling with the controls of the huge, fancy silver grill Travis had splurged on a few months before his death.

She was dressed in a fleece jacket, jeans and boots, with her hair loose and curling around her shoulders. His chest ached at the sight of her, like it always did. He wished, more than anything, that he had the right to go up behind her, brush her hair out of the way and kiss the back of that slender neck.

Little multicolored twinkly Christmas lights covered all the shrubs around the deck and had been draped around the edges of the roof. He didn't remember seeing Christmas lights back here and wondered if Hope had done it to make the rear of the house look more festive. It did look over The Christmas Ranch, after all.

Faith wasn't the biggest fan of Christmas, which he found quite ironic, considering she was part owner of the largest seasonal attraction in these parts.

She fiddled with the knobs again, then smacked the front of the grill. "Why won't you light, you stupid thing?"

"Yelling at it probably won't help much."

She whirled around at his comment and he watched as delectable color soaked her cheeks. "Chase! Oh, I'm so glad to see you!"

He was aware of a fierce, deep-seated need to have her say those words because she wanted to see *him*, not because she had a problem for him to solve.

"Mary said you're having grill trouble."

"The darn thing won't ignite, no matter what I do. It's not getting propane, for some reason. I've been out here for ten minutes trying to figure it out. It's a brand-new tank that Flynn got for us a few weeks ago and we haven't used it since. I checked the propane tank. I tried dropping a match in case it was the ignition. I tried all the knobs about a thousand times. I just think this grill hates me."

He found it more than a little amusing that she had learned to drive every piece of complicated farm machinery on the place over the last two years and could round up a hundred head of cattle on her own, with only the dogs for help, but she was intimidated by a barbecue grill.

"This one can be finicky, that's for sure."

She frowned at the thing. "Travis had to buy the biggest, most expensive grill he could order—forget that the controls on it are more confusing than the space shuttle."

She didn't say disparaging things about her late husband very often. In this case, he had to agree with her. He had loved the guy, but she was absolutely right. Travis Dustin always had to have the best, even when they couldn't afford it. His poor management and expensive tastes in equipment—and his gross negligence in not leaving her with proper life insurance—had all contributed to the big financial hole he had left his family when he died.

"I'll take a look," he said.

She stepped aside and he knelt down to peer at the connection. It only took him a moment to figure out why the grill wouldn't work.

"Here's your trouble. Looks like the gas hose isn't connected tightly. It's come loose from the tank."

He made the necessary adjustment, then stood, turned on the propane and hit the ignition. The grill ignited with a whoosh of instant heat.

She made a face. "Now I feel like an idiot. I swear I checked that already."

"It's easy to overlook."

"I guess my mind must have been on something else."

He had to wonder what. Was she remembering that kiss, too? He cast her a sidelong look and found a pink tinge on her cheeks again that might have been a blush—or just as easily might have been from the cold.

"Thank you for figuring it out," she said.

"No problem. You'll need to let the grill heat up for about ten minutes, then I can come back and take care of the steaks."

"Thank you. No matter how well I think I know my way around all the appliances in my kitchen, apparently this finicky grill remains my bugaboo. Or maybe it's outdoor cookery in general."

"I can't agree with that. I seem to remember some mean Dutch oven meals where you acted as camp cook when Trav and I would combine forces for roundup in the fall."

"That seems like a long time ago."

"Not that long. I still dream about your peach cobbler." Usually his dreams involved her kissing him between thick, gooey spoonfuls, but he decided it would probably be wise not to add that part.

Still, something of his thoughts must have appeared on his face because she seemed to catch her breath and gazed wide-eyed at him in the multicolored glow from the Christmas lights.

"I didn't know you liked it that much," she said after a moment, her voice a little husky. "Dutch oven cooking is easy compared to working this complicated grill. I'll be happy to make you a peach cobbler this summer, when the fruit is in season."

"Sounds delicious," he answered, his own voice a little more gruff than usual, which he told himself was because of the cold—though right now he was much warmer than he might have expected.

She swallowed hard and he was almost positive her gaze drifted to his mouth and then quickly away again. He *was* sure the color on her cheeks intensified, which had to be from more than the cold.

*Was* she remembering that kiss, too? He wanted to ask her—or better yet, to step forward and steal another one, but the door from the house opened and Louisa popped her head out.

"Hey, Chase! Where's Addie? Didn't she come with you?"

He took a subtle step back. "No. She went back to Boise with her mom this afternoon. Didn't she tell you?"

Her face fell. "Oh, no! Does that mean she won't be able to do the show with us? She thought she could! She and I and Olivia were going to sing a song together!"

"She still wants to. She'll have to miss the first few rehearsals, but she should be here next week for the actual show. We'll do our best to get her back here for rehearsal by Thursday. I might have to run into Boise to make it happen."

"Isn't that your day to help out at Jim Laird's place?"

Rats. He had forgotten all about that. "Yes. I'll figure out a way to swing it."

"I'll help," she said promptly. "I can either run to Boise for you or take your day at Jim's house. Either way, we will get Addie here."

His heart twisted a little that with everything she had to do here at the Star N, she would even consider driving six hours round-trip to pick up his daughter.

"Thank you, but I think I can manage both. If I take off as soon as I finish feeding my stock and his, I should be able to have Addie back in time for practice. It's important to her so I'll figure out a way to make it happen."

Both Faith and her daughter gave him matching warm looks that made him forget all about the snow just beyond their little covered patio.

"Thanks, Chase. You're the *best*," Lou said. Despite the cold, she padded out to the deck in her stocking feet and threw her arms around his waist. He smiled a little and hugged her back, thinking how much he loved both Louisa and her brother. They were great kids, always thinking of others. They were like their mother in that respect.

"Better head back inside. It's cold out here and you don't have shoes or a coat."

"I do have to go back in. I have to finish dessert. I made it myself. Aunt Mary hardly helped at all."

"I can't wait," he assured her.

She grinned and skipped back into the house, leaving him alone again with Faith. When he turned away from the doorway, he found her watching him with an expression he couldn't read.

"What did I say?" he asked.

"I... Nothing," she mumbled. "I'll go get the steaks."

She hurried past him before he could press her, leaving him standing alone in the cold.

## Chapter Nine

Faith couldn't leave the intimacy of the covered deck quickly enough.

She felt rattled and unsettled and she hated it. With a deep sense of longing, she remembered dinner just the previous Sunday, when they had laughed and joked and teased like always. He had stayed to watch a movie and she had thrown popcorn into his mouth and teased him about not shaving for a few days.

There had been none of this tension, this awareness that seemed to hiss and flare between them like that stupid grill coming to life.

She had wanted him to kiss her. It was all she could seem to think about, that wondrous feeling of being alive, desired.

Another few moments and she would have been the one to kiss him.

She forced herself to move away from the door and into the kitchen, where Aunt Mary looked up from the rolls she was pulling apart.

"Tell me Chase saved the day again."

"We're in business. It was all about the gas connection. I feel stupid I didn't look there first."

"Sometimes it takes an outside set of eyes to identify the problem and find the solution."

Could someone outside her particular situation help her figure out how to go back in time and fix what felt so very wrong between her and Chase?

"Where are the steaks?" she asked her aunt.

"Over there, by the microwave."

"Whoa," she exclaimed when she spotted them. "That's a lot of steak for just us."

"I took out a few extras in case we had company or so we could use the leftovers for fajitas one day this week. Good thing, because Rafe and Hope said they're only about fifteen minutes out. I'm sure glad they'll beat the worst of the snow. I feel a big storm coming on."

"The weather forecast said most of the storm will clip us."

"Weather forecasts can be wrong. Don't be surprised if we get hit with heavy winds, too."

She had learned not to doubt her great-aunt's intuition when it came to winter storms. After a lifetime of living in this particular corner of Idaho, Mary could read the weather like some people read stock reports.

Sure enough, the wind had already picked up a little

when she carried the tray of steaks out to the covered deck. Chase stood near the propane heater, frowning as he checked something on his phone.

"Trouble?" she asked, nodding at the phone.

"Just Cindy," he answered, his voice terse.

"I'm sorry."

He made a face as he took the tray from her and used the tongs to transfer the steaks onto the grill.

"Nothing new," he said as the air filled with sizzle and scent. "Apparently Addie sulked all the way to Boise about having to go back when she was expecting to stay through the week with me and practice for the show with Olivia and Lou. Of course Cindy blames me. I shouldn't have gotten her hopes up, etc. etc.—even though *she* was the one who changed her mind from her original plan."

Faith wanted to smack the woman. Why did she have to be so difficult?

"Maybe you should petition again for primary custody."

He sighed. "She would never agree. I don't know if that would be the best thing for Addie anyway. Her mom and stepfather have given her a good life in Boise. I just wish she could be closer."

She decided not to tell him about her conversation with Addie the previous morning. What a difficult situation for everyone involved. Her heart ached and she wished, more than anything, that she could give him more time with his daughter for Christmas.

He was such a good man, kind and generous. He

deserved to be happy—which was yet another reason she needed to help him find someone like Ella Baker.

That was what a true friend would do, help him find someone whose heart was whole and undamaged, who could cherish all the wonderful things about him.

Some of her emotions must have appeared on her features because he gave her an apologetic look. "Sorry. I didn't mean to bring you down."

She mustered a smile. "You didn't. What are friends for, if you can't complain about your ex once in a while?"

"I shouldn't complain about her at all. She's my child's mother and overall she takes excellent care of her. She loves her, too. I have to keep reminding myself of that." He shrugged. "I'm not going to worry about it more tonight. For now, let's just enjoy dinner. And speaking of which, I can handle the steaks from here, if you want to go back inside. That wind is really picking up."

"I was planning on grilling," she protested. "You should be the one to go inside. I can take over, as long as you've got the grill working."

"I don't mind."

"If you go inside now, I bet you could nab a hot roll from Aunt Mary."

"Tempting. But no." He wiggled the utensil in his hand. "I've got the tongs, which gives me all the power."

She gave him a mock glare. "Hand them over."

"Come get them, if you think you're worthy."

He held them over his head, which was way over *her* head.

Despite the cold wind, relief wrapped around her like a warm blanket. He was teasing her, just like normal and for a ridiculous moment, she wanted to weep.

Perhaps they *could* find an even footing, return to their easy, dependable friendship.

"Come on. Give," she demanded. She stretched on tiptoe but the tongs were still completely out of reach.

He grinned. "Is that the best you can do?"

Never one to back down from a challenge, she hopped up and her fingers managed to brush the tongs. So close! She tried again but she forgot the wooden planks of the deck were a bit slippery with cold and condensation. This time when she came down, one boot slid and she stumbled a little.

She might have fallen but before she could, his arms instantly came around her, tongs and all.

They froze that way, with his arms around her and her curves pressed against his hard chest. Their smiles both seemed to freeze and crack apart. Her gaze met his and all the heat and tension she had been carefully shoving down seemed to burst to the surface all over again. His mouth was *right there*. She only had to stand on tiptoe again and press her lips to his.

Yearning, wild and sweet, gushed through her and she was aware of the thick churn of her blood, a low flutter in her stomach.

She hitched in a breath and coiled her muscles to do just that when she heard the creak of the door hinges.

She froze for half a second, then quickly stepped away an instant before Rafe tromped out to the deck.

Her brother-in-law paused and gave them a long, considering look, eyebrows raised nearly to his hairline. He
hesitated briefly before he moved farther onto the deck.

"You people are crazy. Don't you know December in
Idaho isn't the time to be firing up the grill?"

Something was definitely fired up out here. The grill
was only part of it. Her face felt hot, her skin itchy, and
she could only hope she had moved away before Rafe
saw anything—*not* that there had been anything to see.

"Steaks just don't taste the same when you try to
cook them under the broiler," Chase said. "Though the
purist in me would prefer to be cooking them over hot
coals instead of a gas flame."

"You ever tried any of that specialty charcoal?" Rafe
asked. "When I was stationed out of Hawaii, I tried the
Ono coals they use for luaus. Man, that's some good
stuff. Burns hot and gives a nice crisp crust."

"I'll have to try it," Chase said.

"I came to see if you needed help but it looks like
you don't need me. You two appear to have things well
in hand," he said.

Was his phrasing deliberate? Faith wondered, feeling her face heat even more.

"Doing our best," Chase replied blandly.

She decided it would be wise to take the chance to
leave while she could. "Thanks for offering, Rafe. I
actually have a few things I just remembered I have to
do before dinner. It would great if you two could finish up out here."

She rushed into the house and tried to tell herself she
was grateful for the narrow escape.

* * *

Chase took another taste of Aunt Mary's delicious mashed potatoes dripping with creamy, rich gravy, and listened to the conversation ebb and flow around him.

He loved listening to the interactions of Faith and her family. With no siblings of his own, he had always envied the close relationships among them all. They never seemed to run out of things to talk about, from current events to Celeste's recent visit to New York to the progress of Hope's pregnancy.

The conversation was lively, at times intense and heated, and never boring. The sisters might disagree with each other or Mary about a particular topic but they always did so with respect and affection.

It was obvious this was a family that loved each other. The girls' itinerant childhood—and especially the tragedy that had followed—seemed to have forged deep, lasting bonds between Faith and her sisters.

Sometimes they opened their circle to include others. Rafe and his nephew Joey. Flynn and Olivia. Chase.

He could lose this.

If this gamble he was taking—trying to force Faith to let things move to the next level between them— didn't pay off, he highly doubted whether Mary would continue to welcome him to these Sunday dinners he treasured.

Things very well might become irreparably broken between them. His jaw tightened. Some part of him wondered if he might be better off backing down and keeping the status quo, this friendship he treasured.

But then he would see Rafe touch Hope's hand as he

made a point or watch Celeste's features soften when she talked about Flynn and he knew he couldn't let it ride. He wanted to have that with Faith. It was possible; he knew it was. That evening on the deck had only reinforced that she was attracted to him but was fighting it with everything she had.

They could be as happy as Rafe and Hope, Celeste and Flynn. Couldn't she see that?

He had told her he would give her time but even though it had only been a few days, he could feel his patience trickling away. He had waited so long already.

"Who's ready for dessert?" Louisa asked eagerly, as the meal was drawing to a close.

Barrett rolled his eyes. "I haven't even finished my steak. You're just in a hurry because you made it."

"So? I never made a whole cheesecake by myself before. Mom or Aunt Mary always helped me, but I made this one all by myself. I even made the crust."

"I saw it in the kitchen and it looks delicious," Chase assured her. "I can't wait to dig in."

She beamed at him and his heart gave a sharp little ache. This was another reason he didn't want to remain on the edge of Faith's life forever. Louisa and Barrett were amazing kids, despite everything they had been through. He wanted so much to be able to help Faith raise them into the good, kind people they were becoming.

He had no idea what he would do next if she was so afraid to take a chance on a relationship with him that she ended up pushing him out of all of their lives.

He would be lost without them.

He set his fork down, the last piece of delicious steak he had been chewing suddenly losing all its flavor.

He had to keep trying to make her see how good they could all be together, even when the risks of this all-or-nothing roll of the dice scared the hell out of him.

"Okay, do you want chocolate sauce or raspberry?" Lou asked.

He managed a smile. "How about a little of both?"

"Great idea," Mary said. "Think I'll have both, too."

Louisa went around the table taking orders like a server in a fancy restaurant, then she and Olivia headed for the kitchen. When Faith rose to go with them to help, Louisa made her sit back down.

"We can do it," she insisted.

The girls left just as another gust of wind rattled the windows and howled beneath the eaves of the old house. The electricity flickered but didn't go out and he couldn't help thinking how cozy it was in here.

They talked about the record-breaking crowd at The Christmas Ranch that weekend until the girls came back with a tray loaded with slices of cheesecake. They were cut a little crooked and the presentation was a bit messy but nobody seemed to mind.

"This is delicious. The best cheesecake I think I've ever had," Chase said after his first bite, which earned him a huge grin from Louisa.

"It is really excellent," Celeste said. "And I've had cheesecake in New York City, where they know cheese-cake."

Louisa couldn't have looked happier. "Thanks. I'm going to try an apple pie next week."

He couldn't resist darting a glance at Faith and wondered if he would ever be able to eat apple pie again without remembering the cinnamon-sugar taste of her mouth.

She licked her lips, then caught his eyes and her cheeks turned an instant pink that made him suddenly certain she was thinking about the kiss, too.

"That wind is sure blowing up a storm," Rafe commented.

"The last update I heard on the weather said we're supposed to have another half foot of snow before morning," Hope said.

"Yay!" all of the children exclaimed together.

"Maybe we won't have school," Joey said with an unmistakably hopeful note in his voice.

"Yeah!" Barrett exclaimed. "That would be awesome!"

"I wouldn't plan on it," Mary said. "I hate to be a downer but I've lived here most of my life and can tell you they hardly ever close school on account of snow. As long as the buses can run, you'll have school."

"It really depends on the timing of the storm and the kind of snowdrifts it leaves behind," Chase said, not wanting the kids to completely give up hope. "If it's early in the morning before the plows can make it around, you might be in luck."

"We should probably head home before the worst of it hits," Rafe said.

"Same here," Celeste said. "I'm so glad Flynn put new storm windows in that old house this summer."

Flynn had spent six months renovating and adding

on to his late grandmother's old house down the road, a project which had been done just days before their wedding in August.

Chase remembered that lovely ceremony on the banks of the Cold Creek, when the two of them—so very perfect for each other—had both glowed with happiness.

Watching them together had only reinforced his determination to forge his own happy ending with Faith, no matter what it took. He had spent the past few months touching her more in their regular interactions, teasing her, trying anything he could think of to convince her to think of him as more than just her friend and confidant.

Right now he felt further from that goal than ever.

Sometimes their Sunday evening dinners would stretch long into the night when they would watch a movie or play games at the kitchen table, but with the storm, everyone seemed in a hurry to leave. They stayed only long enough to clean up the kitchen and then only he, Mary, Faith and her children were left.

"How's the homework situation?" Faith asked from her spot at the kitchen sink drying dishes, a general question aimed at both of her children.

"I had a math work sheet but I finished it on the bus on the way home from school Friday," Louisa said. Chase wasn't really surprised. She was a conscientious student who rarely left schoolwork until Sunday evening.

"How about you, Barrett?"

"I'm almost done. I just had a few problems in math

and they're *hard*. I can ask my teacher tomorrow. We might not even have school anyway so maybe I won't have to turn them in until Tuesday."

"Let's take a look at them," Chase said.

Barrett groaned a little but went to his room for his backpack.

"You don't have to do that," Faith said.

"I don't mind," he assured her.

They sat together at the desk in the great room while the Christmas lights glowed on the tree and a fire flickered in the fireplace. It wasn't a bad way to spend a Sunday night.

After only three or four problems, a lightbulb seemed to switch on in the boy's head—as it usually did.

"Oh! I get it now. That's easy."

"I told you it was."

"It wasn't easy the way my teacher explained it. Why can't you be my teacher?"

He tried not to shudder at the suggestion. "I'm afraid I've already got a job."

"And you're good at it," Mary offered from the chair where she sat knitting.

"Thanks, Mary. I do my best," he answered humbly. He loved being a rancher and wanted to think he was a responsible one.

Now that the boy seemed to be in the groove with his homework, Chase lifted his head from the book and suddenly spotted Faith in the mudroom, putting on her winter gear. He had been so busy helping Barrett, he hadn't noticed.

"Where are you off to? Not out into that wind, I hope."

"I just need to make sure the tarp over the outside haystack is secure. Oh, and check on Rosie," she said, referring to one of her border collies. "She was acting strangely this morning, which makes me think she might be close to having her puppies. I've been trying to keep her in the barn but she wanders off. Before the storm front moves in, I want to be sure she's warm and safe."

Chase scraped his chair back. "I'll come with you."

"You don't need to. You just spent a half hour working on Barrett's homework. I'm sure you've got things to worry about at your place."

He couldn't think of anything. He generally tried to keep things in good order, addressing problems when they came up. He always figured he couldn't go wrong following his father's favorite adage: an ounce of prevention was worth a pound of cure. Better to stop trouble before it could start.

"I'll help," he said. "I'll check the hay cover while you focus on Rosie."

Her mouth tightened for an instant but she finally nodded and waited while he threw his coat on, then together they walked out into the storm.

Darkness came early this time of year near the winter solstice but a few high-wattage electric lights on poles lit their way. The wind howled viciously already and puffed out random snowflakes at them, hard as sharp pebbles.

Below the ranch house, he could see that the parking lot of The Christmas Ranch—which had been full when he pulled up—was mostly cleared out now, with a horse-drawn sleigh on what was probably its last go-round of the evening making its way back to the barn near the lodge.

He would really like to find time before Christmas to take Addie on a ride, along with Faith and her children.

The Saint Nicholas Lodge glowed cheerily against the cold night. Beyond it, the cluster of small structures that made up the life-size Christmas village—complete with indoor animatronic scenes of elves hammering and Santa eating from a plate of cookies—looked like something from a Christmas card.

Her family had created a celebration of the holidays here, unlike anything else in the region. People came from miles around, eager to enhance their holiday spirit.

"It's nice that Hope has hired enough staff now that she doesn't have to do everything on her own," he said.

"With the baby coming, Rafe insisted she cut back her hours. No more fourteen-hour days, seven days a week from Thanksgiving to New Year's."

Those hours were probably not unlike what Faith did year-round on the Star N—at least during calving and haying season and roundup. In other words, most of the year.

She worked so hard and never complained about the burden that had fallen onto her shoulders after Travis died.

When they reached the haystack, tucked beneath a huge open-sided structure with a metal roof, he heard the problem before he saw it, the thwack of a loose tarp cover flapping in the wind. Each time the wind dug underneath the tarp, it pulled it loose a little further. If they didn't tie it down, it would eventually pull the whole thing loose and she would not only lose an expensive tarp but potentially the whole haystack to the storm.

"That's gotten a lot worse, just in the last few hours," she said, pitching her voice louder to be heard over the wind. "I should have taken time to fix it earlier when I first spotted the problem, but I was doing about a hundred other things at the time. I was going to fix it in the morning, but I didn't take into account the storm."

"It's fine," he said. "We'll have it safe and secure in no time. It might take both of us, though—one to hold the flap down and hold the flashlight while the other ties it."

They went to work together, as they had done a hundred times before. He wrestled the tarp down, which wasn't easy amid the increasing wind, then held it while she tied multiple knots to keep it in place.

"That should do it," she said.

"While we're out here, let's tighten the other corners," he suggested.

When he was satisfied the tarp was secure—and when the bite of the wind was close to becoming uncomfortable—he tightened the last knot.

"Thanks, Chase," she said.

"No problem. Let's go see if Rosie is smart enough to stay in from the cold."

She clutched at her hat to keep the wind from tugging it away and they made their way into the relative warmth and safety of her large, clean barn.

The wind still howled outside but it was muted, more like a low, angry buzz, making the barn feel like a refuge.

"That wind has to be thirty or forty miles an hour," she said, shaking her head as she turned on the lights inside the barn.

"At least this storm isn't supposed to bring bitter cold along with it," he said. "Where's Rosie?"

"I set her up in the back stall but who knows if she decided to stay put? I really hope she's not out in that wind somewhere."

Apparently the dog knew this cozy spot was best for her and her pups. They found her lying on her side on an old horse blanket with five brand-new white-and-black puppies nuzzling at her.

"Oh. Will you look at that?" Faith breathed. Her eyes looked bright and happy in the fluorescent barn lights. "Hi there, Rosie. Look at you! What a good girl. Five babies. Good job, little mama!"

She leaned on the top railing of the stall and he joined her. "The kids will be excited," he observed.

"Are you kidding? *Excited* is an understatement. Puppies for Christmas. They'll be thrilled. If I let her, Louisa probably would be down here in a minute and want to spend the night right there in the straw with Rosie."

The dog flapped her tail at the sound of her name and they watched for a moment before he noticed her water bowl was getting low. He slipped inside the stall and picked up the food and the water bowls and filled them each before returning them to the cozy little pen.

For his trouble, he earned another tail wag from
Rosie and a smile from Faith.

"Thank you. Do you think they'll be warm enough
out here? I can take them into the house."

"They should be okay. She might not appreciate
being moved now. They're warm enough in here and
they're out of the wind. If you're really worried about
it, I can bring over a warming lamp."

"That's a good idea, at least for the first few days.
I've got one here. I should have thought of that."

She headed to another corner of the barn and returned a moment later with the large lamp and they
spent a few moments hanging it from the top beam of
the stall.

"Perfect. That should do the trick."

While the wind howled outside, they stood for a
while watching the dog and her pups beneath the glow
of the heat lamp. He wasn't in a big hurry to leave this
quiet little scene and he sensed Faith wasn't either.

"Seems like just a minute ago that she was a pup herself," she said in a soft voice. "I guess it's been a while,
though. Three years. She was in the last litter we had
out of Lillybelle, so she would have been born just a
few months before Travis..."

Her voice broke off and she gazed down at the puppies with her mouth trembling a little.

"Life rolls on," he said quietly.

"Like it or not, I guess," she answered after a moment. "Thanks for your help tonight, first with Barrett's

homework and then with storm preparation. You're too good to us."

"You know I'm always happy to help."

"You shouldn't be," she whispered.

He frowned. "Shouldn't be what?"

She kept her attention fixed on the wriggling puppies. "Celeste gave me a lecture the other night. She told me I'm not being fair to you. She said I take you for granted."

"We're friends. Friends help each other. You feed me every Sunday and usually more often than that. Addie practically lives over here when I have visitation and also ranch work I can't avoid. And you bought my groceries the other day, right?"

"Don't forget to take them home when you go." She released a heavy sigh. "We both know the ledger will never be balanced, no matter how many groceries I buy for you. The Star N wouldn't have survived without you. I don't know why you are so generous with your time and energy on our behalf but I hope you know how very grateful we are. How very grateful *I* am. Thank you. And I hope you know how…how much we all love you."

He looked down at her, wondering at the murky subtext he couldn't quite read here.

"I'm happy to help out," he answered again.

She swallowed hard, avoiding his gaze. "I guess what I wanted to tell you is that things are better now. The Star N is back in the black, thanks in large part to you and to The Christmas Ranch finally being self-sustaining. I'll never been an expert at ranching but I kind of feel like

I know a little more what I'm doing now. If you…want to ease away a bit so you can focus more on your own ranch, I would completely understand. Don't worry. We'll be fine."

It took about two seconds for him to go from confusion to being seriously annoyed.

"So you're basically telling me you don't want me hanging around anymore."

She looked instantly horrified. "No! That's not what I'm saying at all. I just…don't want you to feel obligated to do as much as you have for us. For me. I needed help and would have been lost without you the last two years but you can't prop us up forever. At some point, I have to stand on my own."

"Would you be saying this if I hadn't kissed you the other night?"

Her eyes widened and she looked startled that he had brought the kiss up when they both had been so carefully avoiding the subject.

Finally she sighed. "I don't know," she said, her voice low again and her gaze fixed on the five little border collie puppies. "It feels like everything has changed."

She sounded so miserable, he wanted to pull her into his arms and tell her he was sorry, that he would do his best to make sure things returned to the way they were a week ago.

"Life has a way of doing that, whether we always like it or not," he said, knowing full well he wouldn't go back, even if he could. "Nobody escapes it. The trick is figuring out how to roll with the changes."

She was silent for a long time and he would have given anything to know what she was thinking.

When she spoke, her voice was low. "I can't stop thinking about that kiss."

## Chapter Ten

At first he wasn't sure he heard her correctly or if his own subconscious had conjured the words out of nowhere.

But then he looked at her and her eyes were solemn, intense and more than a little nervous.

He swallowed hard. "Same here. It's all I could think about during dinner. I would like, more than anything, to kiss you again."

She opened her mouth as if she wanted to object. He waited for it, bracing himself for yet one more disappointment. To his utter shock, she took a step forward instead, placed her hands against his chest and lifted her face in clear invitation.

He didn't hesitate for an instant. How could he? He wasn't a stupid man. He framed her face with his hands, then lowered his mouth, brushing against hers once, twice. Her mouth was cool, her lips trembling, and she tasted of raspberry and chocolate from Louisa's cheesecake—rich, heady. Irresistible.

At first she seemed nervous, unsure, but after only a moment, her hands slid around his neck and she pressed against him, surrendering to the heat swirling between them.

He was awash in tenderness, completely enamored with the courageous woman in his arms.

Optimism bubbled up inside him, a tiny trickle at first, then growing stronger as she sighed against his mouth and returned his kiss with a renewed enthusiasm that took his breath away. For the first time in days, he began to think that maybe, just maybe, she was beginning to see that this was real, that they were perfect together.

They kissed for several delicious moments, until his breathing was ragged and he wanted nothing more than to find a soft pile of straw somewhere, lower her down and show her exactly how amazing things could be between them.

A particularly fierce gust of wind rattled the windows of the barn, distracting him enough to realize a cold, drafty barn that smelled of animals and hay might not be the most romantic of spots.

With supreme effort, he forced his mouth to slide away from hers, pressing his forehead to hers and giving them both a chance to collect their breath and their thoughts.

Her eyes were dazed, aroused. "I feel like I've been

asleep for nearly three years and now...I'm not," she admitted.

He pressed a soft kiss on her mouth again. "Welcome back."

She smiled a little but it slid away too soon, replaced by an anxious expression, and she took another step away. He wanted to tug her back into his arms but he knew he couldn't kiss her into accepting the possibilities between them, as tempting as he found that idea.

"I'm afraid," she admitted.

His growing optimism cooled like the air that rushed between them. "Of what? I hope you know I would rather stab myself in the foot with a pitchfork than ever hurt you."

"Maybe I don't want to hurt *you*," she whispered, her features distressed. "You're the best man I know, Chase. When I think about...about not having you in my life, I feel like I'm going to throw up. But I'm not sure I'm ready for this again—or that I ever will be."

Well. That was honest enough. He had to respect it, even if he didn't like it. It took him a moment to grab his scrambled thoughts and formulate them into something he hoped came out coherently.

"That's a decision you'll have to make," he said, choosing his words with care. "But think about those puppies. We can keep them here under that heat lamp forever where it's safe and warm and dry. That's the best place for them right now, I agree, while they're tiny and vulnerable. But they won't always be the way they are right now, and what kind of existence would those puppies have if they could never really have the chance to experience the world? They're meant to run across fields and chase birds and lie stretched out in the summer sunshine. To live."

She let out a breath. "You're comparing me to those puppies."

"I'm only saying I understand you've suffered a terrible loss. I know how hard you've fought to work through the grief. It's only natural to want to protect yourself, to be afraid of moving out of the safe place you've created for yourself out of that grief."

"Terrified," she admitted.

His heart ached for her and the struggle he had forced on her. He wanted to reach for her hands but didn't trust himself to touch her right now. "I can tell you this, Faith. You have too much love inside you to spend the rest of your life hiding inside that safe haven while the world moves on without you."

Her gaze narrowed. "That's easy for you to say. You never lost someone you loved with all your heart."

He wanted to tell her he *had*, only in a different way. He had lost her over and over again—though could a guy really lose what he'd never had?

"You're right. I can only imagine," he lied.

As tempting as it was to tell her everything in his heart—that he had loved her since that afternoon he took her shopping for Aunt Mary—he didn't dare. Not yet. Something told him that would send her running away even faster.

She would have to be the one to make the decision about whether she was ready to open her heart again.

The storm rattled the window again, fierce and demanding, and she shivered suddenly, though he couldn't tell if it was from the cold or from the emotional winds battering them. Either way, he didn't want her to suffer.

"Let's get you back to the house. Mary will be wondering where we are."

She nodded. After one more check of the puppies, she tugged her gloves back on and headed out into the night.

Faith was fiercely aware of him as they walked from the barn to the ranch house with the wind and snow howling around them.

She felt as if all the progress she had made toward rebuilding her world had been tossed out into this storm. She had been so proud of herself these last few months. The kids were doing well, the ranch was prospering, she had finally developed a new routine and had begun to be more confident in what she was doing.

While she wouldn't say she had been particularly happy, at least she had found some kind of acceptance with her new role as a widow. She was more comfortable in her own skin.

Now she felt as if everything had changed again. Once more she was confused, off balance, not sure how to put one more step in front of the other and forge a new path.

She didn't like it.

Even in the midst of her turmoil, she couldn't miss the way he placed his body in the path of the wind to protect her from the worst of it. That was so much like

Chase, always looking out for her. It warmed her heart, even as it made her ache.

"You still need your groceries," she said when they reached the house. "Come in and I'll grab them."

He looked as if he had something more to say but he finally nodded and followed her inside.

Though she could hear the television playing down the hall in the den, the kitchen was dark and empty. A clean, vacant kitchen on Sunday night after the big family party always left her feeling a little bereft, for some strange reason.

She flipped on the light and discovered a brown paper bag on the counter with his name on it. She couldn't resist peeking inside and discovered it contained a half dozen of the dinner rolls. Knowing Aunt Mary and her habits, she pulled open the refrigerator and found another bag with his name on it.

"It looks like Mary saved some leftovers for you."

"Excellent. It will be nice not having to worry about dinner tomorrow."

She knew he rarely cooked when Addie was with her mother, subsisting on frozen meals, sandwiches and the occasional steaks he grilled in a batch. Mary knew it, too, which might be another reason she invited him over so often.

Faith headed to the walk-in pantry where she had left the things she bought at the store for him.

"Here you go. Dishwashing detergent, dish soap and paper towels."

"That should do it. Thanks for picking them up for me."

"It was no trouble at all."

"I'll check in with you first thing in the morning to see if you had any storm damage."

If she were stronger, she would tell him thank you but it wasn't necessary. At some point in a woman's life, she had to figure out how to clean up her own messes. Instead, she did her best to muster a smile. "Be careful driving home."

He nodded. Still looking as if he had something more to say, he headed for the door. He put a hand on the knob but before he could turn it, he whirled back around, stalked over to her and kissed her hard with a ferocity and intensity that made her knees so weak she had to clutch at his coat to keep from falling.

She could only be grateful none of her family members came into the kitchen just then and stumbled over them.

When he pulled away, a muscle in his jaw worked but he only looked at her out of solemn, intense eyes.

"Good night," he said.

She didn't have the breath to speak, even if she trusted herself to say anything, so she only nodded.

The moment he left, she pulled her ranch coat off with slow, painstaking effort, hung it in the mudroom, then sank down into a kitchen chair, fighting the urge to bury her face in her hands and weep.

She felt like the world's biggest idiot.

She knew she relied on him, that he had become her rock and the core of her support system since Travis died. He made her laugh and think, he challenged her, he praised her when things went well and held her when they didn't.

All this time, when she considered him her dearest friend, some part of her already knew the feelings she had for him ran deeper than that.

She felt so stupid that it had taken her this long to figure it out. She had always known she loved him, just as she had told him earlier.

She had just never realized she was also *in love* with him.

How had it happened? How could she have *let* it happen?

She should have known something had shifted over the last few months when she started anticipating the times she knew she would see him with a new sort of intensity, when she became more aware of the way other women looked at him when they were together, as she started noticing a ripple of muscle, the solid strength of him as he did some ordinary task in the barn.

She should have realized, but it all just seemed so... natural.

She was still sitting there trying to come to terms with the shock when Mary came into the kitchen wearing her favorite flannel nightgown over long underwear and thick socks.

"Did Chase take off? I had leftovers for him."

She summoned a smile that felt a little wobbly at the edges. "He took them. Don't worry."

"Oh, you know me. Worrying is what I do best." Mary looked out the window where the snow lashed in hard pellets. "I'll tell you, I don't like him driving into the teeth of that nasty wind. All it would take would be one tree limb to fall on his pickup truck."

Her heart clutched at the unbearable thought.

This. This was why she couldn't let herself love him. She would not survive losing a man she loved a second time.

She pushed the grim fear away, choosing instead to focus on something positive.

"Rosie had her puppies. Five of them."

"Is that right?" Mary looked pleased.

"They're adorable. I'm sure the kids will want to see them first thing."

"I made them take their showers for the night. Barrett isn't very happy with me right now but I'm sure he'll get over it. They're both in their rooms, reading."

She would go read to them in a moment. It was her favorite part of the day, those quiet moments when she could cuddle her children and explore literary worlds with them. "Thank you," she said to her aunt. "I don't tell you enough how much I appreciate your help."

Mary sat down across from her at the table. "Are you okay? You seem upset."

For a moment, she desperately wanted to confide in her beloved great-aunt, who was just about the wisest person she knew. The words wouldn't come, though. Mary wouldn't be an unbiased observer in this particular case as Mary adored Chase and always had.

"I'm just feeling a little down tonight."

Mary took Faith's hands in her own wrinkled, age-spotted ones. "I get that way sometimes. The holidays sure make me feel alone."

A hard nugget of guilt lodged in her chest. She wasn't the only one in the world who had ever suffered heartache. Uncle Claude had died five years earlier and they all still missed him desperately.

"You're not alone," she told her aunt. "You've got us, as long as you want us."

"I know that, my dear, and I can't tell you how grateful I am for that." Mary squeezed her fingers. "It's not quite the same. I miss my Claude."

She thought of her big, burly, white-haired greatuncle, who had adored Christmas so much that he had started The Christmas Ranch with one small herd of reindeer to share his love of the holiday with the community.

"I'm thinking about dating again," Mary announced. "What do you think?"

She blinked at that completely unexpected piece of information. "Really?"

"Why not? Your uncle's been gone for years and I'm not getting any younger."

"I... No. You're not. I think it's great. Really great."

Her aunt made a face. "I don't know about *great*. More like a necessary evil. I'd like to get married again, have a companion in my old age, and unfortunately you usually have to go through the motions and go on a few dates first in order to get there."

Her seventy-year-old great-aunt was braver than she was. It was another humbling realization. "Do you have someone in mind?"

Her aunt shrugged. "A couple of widowers at the senior citizens center have asked me out. They're nice enough, but I was thinking about asking Pat Walters out to dinner."

She tried not to visibly react to yet another stunner. For years, Pat had been one of the men who played Santa Claus at The Christmas Ranch. His wife had died just a few months after Uncle Claude.

She digested the information and the odd *rightness* of the idea.

"You absolutely should," she finally said. "He's a great guy."

"He is. Truth is, we went out a few times three years ago when I was living in town and we had a lot of fun together. I didn't tell you girls because it was early days yet and there was nothing much to tell."

She shrugged her ample shoulders. "But then Travis died and I moved back in here to help you with the kids. I just didn't feel like the time was right to complicate things so Pat and I put things on the back burner for a while."

Oh, the guilt. The nugget turned into a full-on boulder. Had she really been so wrapped up in her own pain that she hadn't noticed a romance simmering right under her nose?

What else had she missed?

"I wish you had told me," she said. "I hate that you put your life on hold for me. I would have been okay. Celeste was here to help me out in the evenings and I could have hired someone to help me with Lou and Barrett when I was busy on the ranch and couldn't take them with me."

Mary frowned. "I didn't tell you about Pat to make you feel guilty. You didn't force me to move in after

Travis died. You didn't even *ask* me. I did it because I needed to, because that's what family does for each other."

Mary and Claude had been helping her and her sisters for eighteen years, since they had been three traumatized, frightened, grieving girls.

Her aunt, with her quiet strength, support and wisdom, had been a lifesaver to her after her parents died and even more of one after Travis died.

"I can never repay you for everything you've done," she said, her throat tight and the hot burn of tears behind her eyes.

Mary sat back in her chair and skewered her with a stern look. "Is that what you think I want? For you to repay me?"

"Of course! I wish I could."

"Well, you're right. I do."

She blinked. "Okay."

"You can do that by showing me I taught you a thing or two over the years about surviving and thriving, even when the going is tough."

She stared at her aunt, wondering where this was coming from. "I... What do you mean?"

"Life isn't meant to be lived in fear, honey," Mary said.

It was so similar to her recent conversation with Chase that she had to swallow. "I know."

"Do you?" Mary pressed. "I'm just saying. Chase won't wait around for you forever, you know."

Faith pulled her hands from her aunt's and curled

them into fists on her lap. "I don't know what you mean."

Mary snorted. "Of the three of you, you were always the worst liar. You know exactly what I mean. That boy is in love with you and has been forever."

She felt hot and then ice-cold. First Celeste, now Aunt Mary. What had they seen that she had missed all this time?

She wanted to protest but even in her head, any counterargument she tried to formulate sounded stupid and trite. Was it true? Had he been in love with her and had she been so preoccupied with life that she hadn't realized?

Or worse, much worse, had she realized it on some subconscious level and simply taken it for granted all this time?

"Chase is my best friend, Mary. He's been like a father to the kids since Travis died. And you and I both know we would have had to sell the ranch if he hadn't helped me pull it back from the brink."

Her aunt gave her a hard look. "Seems to me there are worse things to base a relationship on. Not to mention, he's one good-looking son of a gun."

She couldn't deny that. And he kissed like a dream.

"I'm so scared," she whispered.

Mary made that snorting noise again. "Who isn't, honey? If you're not scared sometimes, you're just plain stupid. The trick is to decide how much of your life you're willing to sacrifice for those fears."

Before she could come up with an answer, her aunt

rose. "I'm going to turn in and you've got kids waiting for you to read to them."

She rose, as well. "Thank you, Mary."

She didn't know if she was thanking her for the advice or the last eighteen years of wisdom. She supposed it didn't really matter.

Her aunt hugged her. "Don't worry. You'll figure it out. Good night, honey. Sleep well."

She would have laughed if she thought she could pull it off without sounding hysterical.

Something told her more than the wind would be keeping her up that night.

She didn't see Chase at all the next week. Maybe he was only giving her space, as she had asked, or maybe he was as busy at his place as she was at the Star N, trying to finish up random jobs before the holidays.

Or maybe he was finally fed up with her cowardice and indecision.

Though she didn't see him, she did talk to him on the phone twice.

He called her once on Monday morning, the day after the storm and that stunning kiss in the barn, to make sure her ranch hadn't sustained significant damage from the winds and snows.

On Thursday afternoon, he called to tell her he was driving to Boise to pick up Addie a day earlier than planned and asked if she needed him to bring anything back from Boise for the kids' stockings.

He had sounded distant and frazzled. She knew how tough it was for him to be separated from Addie over the holidays, which made his thoughtfulness in worrying about Louisa and Barrett even more touching.

Again, she wanted to smack Cindy for her selfishness in booking a cruise over the holidays without consulting him.

He could have withheld permission and the court would have sided with him. After Cindy sprang the news on him, though, he had told Faith he hadn't wanted to drag Addie into a war between her parents.

As a result, he was planning their own Christmas celebration a few days before the actual holiday, complete with Christmas Eve dinner, presents and all.

"I think we're covered," she told him, her heart aching. "Be careful driving back. Oh, and let Addie know she's still on to sing with Louisa and Olivia. Ella is planning on it."

"I'll tell her. She'll be thrilled. Thanks."

She wanted to tell him so many other things. That she hadn't stopped thinking about him. That their kisses seemed to play through her head on an endless loop. That she just needed a little more time. She couldn't find the courage to say any of it so he ended up telling her goodbye rather abruptly and severing the connection.

There had been times when they stayed on the phone the entire time he drove to Boise to pick up his daughter, never running out of things to talk about.

Were those days gone forever?

She sighed now and headed toward Saint Nicholas Lodge with a couple of letters that had been delivered to the main house by accident, probably because the post office had temporary help handling the holiday mail volume.

Though she waved at the longtime clerk at the gift store, she didn't stop to chat, heading straight for the office instead, where she found Hope sitting behind her desk.

"Mail delivery," Faith announced, setting the letters on the desk. "It looks like a bill for reindeer food and one for candy canes. I might have a tough time convincing my accountant those are legitimate expenses for a cattle ranch."

When Hope didn't reply, Faith's gaze sharpened on her sister. Fear suddenly clutched her when she registered her sister's pale features, her pinched mouth, the haunted eyes. "What is it, honey? What's wrong?"

"Oh, Faith. I... I was just about to call you."

Her sister's last word ended in a sob that she tried to hide but Faith wasn't fooled. She also suddenly realized her sister's arms were crossed protectively across her abdomen.

"What's wrong? Is it the baby?"

Hope nodded, tears dripping down the corners of her eyes. "I've been having crampy aches all day and I... I just don't feel good. I was just in the bathroom and...had some spotting. Oh, Faith. I'm afraid I'm losing the baby."

She burst into tears and Faith instantly went to her side and wrapped her arms around her. Her younger sister was normally so controlled in any crisis. Even when they had been kidnapped, Hope had been calm and cool.

Seeing her lose it like this broke Faith's heart in two.

"What do you need me to do? I can call Rafe. I can run you into the doctor's. Whatever you need."

"I just called Rafe." Hope wiped at her eyes, though she continued to weep. "He's on his way and we're running into Jake Dalton's office. It might be nothing. I might be overreacting. I hope so."

"I do, too." She whispered a prayer that her sister could endure whatever outcome.

She wouldn't let herself focus on the worst, thinking instead about what a wonderful mother Hope would be. She was made for it. She loved children and had spent much of her adult life following their parents' examples and trying to help those in need around the world in her own way.

Really, coming home and running The Christmas Ranch had been one more way Hope wanted to help people, by giving them a little bit of holiday spirit in a frazzled word.

"It's the worst possible time," Hope said, her eyes distressed. "Within the hour, I've got forty kids showing up to practice for the play."

"That is absolutely the least of your concerns," Faith said, going into big sister mode. "I forbid you to worry about a single thing at The Christmas Ranch. You've got an excellent staff, not to mention a family ready to step in and cover whatever else you might need. Focus on yourself and on the baby. That's an order."

Hope managed a wobbly smile that did nothing to conceal the fear beneath it. "You're always so bossy."

"That's right." She squeezed her sister's fingers.

"And right now I'm ordering you to lie down and wait for your husband, this instant."

Hope went to the low sofa in the office and complied. While she rested, Faith found her sister's coat and her voluminous tote bag and carried them both to her, then sat holding her hand for a few more moments, until Rafe arrived.

He looked as pale as his wife and hugged her tightly, green eyes murky with worry. "Whatever happens, we'll be okay," he assured her.

It took all her strength not to sob at the gentleness of the big, tough former navy SEAL as he all but carried Hope out to his SUV and settled her into the passenger side. Faith handed her the tote bag she had carried along.

"Call me the minute you know anything," she ordered.

"I will. I promise. Faith, can you stay during rehearsals to make sure Ella has everything she needs?"

"Of course."

"Don't tell Barrett and Lou yet. I don't want them to worry."

"Nothing to tell," she said. "Because you and that baby are going to be absolutely fine."

If she kept saying that, perhaps she could make it true.

She watched them drive away, shivering a little until she realized she had left her own coat in Hope's office. Before she could go inside for it, she spotted Chase's familiar pickup truck.

How did he always know when she needed him? she

wondered, then realized he must be dropping Addie off for rehearsal.

She didn't care why he had come. Only that he was there.

She moved across the parking lot without even thinking it through. Desperate for the strength and comfort of his embrace, she barely gave him time to climb out of his vehicle before she was at his side, wrapping her arms tightly around him.

She saw shock and concern flash in his eyes for just an instant before he held her tight against him. "What's going on? What's wrong?" he asked, his voice urgent.

Addie was with him, Faith realized with some dismay. She couldn't burst into tears, not without the girl wondering about it and then telling Lou and Barrett, contrary to Hope's wishes.

"It's Hope," she whispered in his ear. "She's threatening a miscarriage."

He growled a curse that made Addie blink.

"It's too early to know for sure yet," Faith said quietly. "Rafe just took her to the doctor."

"What can I do?"

It was so like him to want to fix everything. The thought would have made her smile if she weren't so very worried. "I don't think we can do anything yet. Just hope and pray she and the baby will both be okay."

"Will she need extra help here at The Christmas Ranch? I can cover you at the Star N if you need to step in here until the New Year."

Oh, the dear man. He was already doing extra work

for their neighbor and now he wanted to add Faith's workload to his pile, as well.

"I hope I don't have to take you up on that but it's too early to say right now."

"Keep me posted."

"I will. I... Thank you, Chase."

"You're welcome."

She would have said more but other children started to arrive and the moment was gone.

## Chapter Eleven

Chase ended up staying to watch the rehearsal, figuring he could help corral kids if need be.

He had plenty of other things he should be doing but nothing else seemed as important as being here if Faith or her family needed him.

A few minutes after the rehearsal started, Celeste showed up. She went immediately to the office, where Faith was staring into space. The two of them embraced, both wiping tears. Not long after, Mary showed up, too, and the three of them sat together, not saying much.

He wanted to go in there but didn't quite feel it was his place so he stayed where he was and watched the children sing about Silver Bells and Holly Jolly Christmases and Silent Nights.

About an hour into rehearsal—when he felt more

antsy than he ever remembered—Faith took a call on her cell phone. The anxiety and fear on her features cut through him and he couldn't resist rising to his feet and going to the doorway.

"Are they sure? Yes. Yes. I understand." Her features softened and she gave a tremulous smile. "That's the best news, Rafe. The absolute best. Thank you for calling. I'll tell them. Yes. Give her all our love and tell her to take care of herself and not to worry about a thing. That's an order. Same goes for you. We love you, too, you know."

She hung up, her smile incandescent, then she gave a little cry that ended on a sob. "Dr. Dalton says for now everything seems okay with the baby. The heartbeat is strong and all indications are good for a healthy pregnancy."

"Oh, thank the Lord," Mary exclaimed.

She nodded and they all spent a silent moment doing just that.

"Jake wants to put her on strict bed rest for the next few weeks to be safe," Faith said after a moment. "That means the rest of us will have to step up here."

"I'm available for whatever you need," Chase offered once more.

She gave him a distracted smile. "I know but, again, you have plenty to do at your own place. We can handle it."

"I want to help." He tried to tamp down his annoyance that she was immediately pushing aside his help.

"We actually could use him tomorrow," Celeste said thoughtfully.

Faith didn't look convinced. "We'll just have to cancel that part of the party, under the circumstances. The kids will have to understand."

"They're kids," her sister pointed out. "They won't understand anything but disappointment."

"I'll just do it, then," Faith said.

"How, when you're supposed to be helping me with everything else?"

He looked from one to the other without the first idea what they were talking about. "What do you need me to do?"

"I've been running a holiday reading contest at the library for the last two months and the children who have read enough pages earned a special party tomorrow at the ranch," Celeste said. "Sparkle is supposed to make an appearance and we also promised the children wagon rides around the ranch. Our regular driver will be busy taking the regular customers to see the lights so Rafe has been practicing with our backup team so he could help out at the party. Obviously, he needs to be with Hope now. Flynn is coming back tomorrow but he won't be here in time to help, even if he learns overnight how to drive a team of draft horses."

Why hadn't they just asked him in the first place? Was it because things with him and Faith had become so damn complicated?

"I can do it, no problem—as long as you don't mind if Addie comes along."

Celeste gave him a grateful smile. "Oh, thank you! And Addie would be more than welcome. She's such a reader she probably would have earned the party anyway. Olivia, Lou and Faith are my volunteer helpers and I'm sure they would love Addie's help."

"Great. I'll plan on it, then. Just let me know what time."

They worked out a few more details, all while he was aware of Faith's stiff expression.

At least he would get to see her the next day, even if she clearly didn't want him there.


She lived in the most beautiful place on earth.

Faith lifted her face to the sky, pale lavender with the deepening twilight. As she drove the backup team of draft horses around the Star N barn so she could take them down to the lodge late Sunday afternoon, the moon was a slender crescent above the jagged Teton mountain range to the east and the entire landscape looked still and peaceful.

Sometimes she had to pinch herself to believe she really lived here.

When she was a girl, she had desperately wanted a place to call her own.

She had spent her entire childhood moving around the world while her parents tried to make a difference. She had loved and respected her parents and understood, even then, that they genuinely wanted to help people as they moved around to impoverished villages setting up medical clinics and providing the training to run them after they left.

She wasn't sure *they* understood the toll their self-ordained missionary efforts were taking on their daughters, even before the terrifying events shortly before their deaths.

Faith hadn't known anything other than their transitory lifestyle. She hadn't blinked an eye at the primitive conditions, the language barriers, making friends only to have to tearfully leave them a few months later.

Still, some part of her had yearned for *this*, though she never had a specific spot in mind. All she had really wanted was a place to call her own, anywhere. A loft in the city, a split-level house in the suburbs, a double-wide mobile home somewhere. She hadn't cared what. She just wanted roots somewhere.

For nearly sixteen years, that had been her secret dream, the one she hadn't dared share with her parents. That dream had become reality only after a series of traumas and tragedies. The kidnapping. The unspeakable ordeal of their month spent in the rebel camp. Her father's shocking death during the rescue attempt, then her mother's cancer diagnosis immediately afterward.

She had been shell-shocked, grieving, frightened out of her mind but trying to put on a brave front for her younger sisters as they traveled to their new home in Idaho to live with relatives they barely knew.

When Claude picked them up at the airport in Boise and drove them here, everything had seemed so strange and new, like they had been thrust into an alien landscape.

Until they drove onto the Star N, anyway.

Faith still remembered the moment they arrived at the ranch and the instant, fierce sense of belonging she had felt.

In the years since, it had never left her. She felt the same way every time she returned to the ranch after spending any amount of time away from it. This was home, each beautiful inch of it. She loved ranching more than she could have dreamed. Whoever would have guessed that she would one day become so comfortable at this life that she could not only hitch up a team of draft horses but drive them, too?

The bells on the horses jingled a festive song as she guided the team toward the shortcut to the Saint Nicholas Lodge. Before she could go twenty feet, she spotted a big, gorgeous man in a black Stetson blocking their way.

"I thought I was the hired driver for the night," Chase called out.

She pulled the horses to a stop and fought down the butterflies suddenly swarming through her on fragile wings.

"I figured I could get them down there for you. Anyway, we just bought new sleigh bells for the backup sleigh and I wanted to try them out."

"They sound good to me."

"I think they'll do. Where's Addie?"

"Down at the lodge, helping Olivia and Lou set things up for the party. We stopped there first and Celeste sent me up here to see if you needed help with the team."

Faith fought a frown. She had a feeling her sister sent him out here as yet another matchmaking ploy. Her family was going to drive her crazy. "I've got things under control," she lied. She was only recently coming to see it wasn't true, in any aspect of her life.

"That's good," he said as he greeted the horses, who were old friends of his. "How's Hope?"

"I checked on her a few hours ago and she is feeling fine. She had a good night and has had no further symptoms today. Looks like the crisis has passed."

In the fading light, she saw stark relief on his chiseled features. "I'm so glad. I've been worried all day. And how is your other little mama?"

It took her a moment to realize he meant Rosie. "All the pups are great. They opened their eyes yesterday. The kids have had so much fun watching them. You'll have to bring Addie over."

"I'll try to do that before she leaves on Wednesday but our schedule's pretty packed between now and then. I don't think we'll even have time for Sunday dinner tomorrow."

"Oh. That's too bad," she said, as he moved away from the horses toward the driver's seat of the sleigh. "The family will miss you."

"What about you?" he asked, his voice low and his expression intense.

She swallowed, not knowing what to say. "Yes," she finally said. "Good thing we're not having steak or we wouldn't know how to light the grill."

"Good thing." He tipped his hat back. "Is there room for me up there or are you going to make me walk back to the lodge?"

She slid over and he jumped up and took the reins she handed him.

Though there was plenty of space on the bench, she immediately felt crowded, fiercely aware of the heat of him beside her.

Maybe *she* ought to walk back to the lodge.

The thought hardly had time to register before he whistled to the horses and they obediently took off down the drive toward the lodge, bells jingling.

After a moment, she forced herself to relax and enjoy the evening. She could think of worse ways to spend an evening than driving across her beautiful land in the company of her best friend, who just happened to be a gorgeous cowboy.

"Wow, what a beautiful night," he said after a few moments. "Hard to believe that less than a week ago we were gearing up for that nasty storm."

"We're not supposed to have any more snow until Christmas Eve."

"With what we already have on the ground, I don't think there's any question that we'll have a white Christmas."

"Who knows? It's Idaho. We could have a heat wave between now and then."

"Don't break out your swimming suit yet," he advised. "Unless you want to take a dip in Carson and Jenna McRaven's pool at their annual party this week."

"Not me. I'm content watching the kids have fun in the pool."

The McRavens' holiday party, which would be the night *after* the show for the senior citizens, had become legendary around these parts, yet another tradition she cherished.

"I don't think I'll be able to make it to that one this year," he said. "It's my last day with Addie."

"You're still doing Christmas Eve the night of the show?"

"That's the plan."

It made her heart ache to think of him getting everything ready for his daughter on his own, hanging out stockings and scattering her presents under the tree.

"You're a wonderful father, Chase," she said softly.

He frowned as the sleigh's movement jostled her against him. "Not really. If I were, I might have tried harder to stay married to her mother. Instead, I've given my daughter a childhood where she feels constantly torn between the both of us."

"You did your best to make things work."

"Did I?"

"It looked that way from the outside."

"I should never have married her. If she hadn't been pregnant with Addie, I wouldn't have."

He was so rarely open about his marriage and divorce that she was momentarily shocked. The cheery jingle bells seemed discordant and wrong, given his serious tone.

"It was a mistake," he went on. "We both knew it. I just hate that Addie is the one who has suffered the most."

"She has a mother and stepfather who love her and a father who adores her. She's a sweet, kind, good-hearted girl. You're doing okay. Better than okay. You're a wonderful father and I won't let you beat yourself up."

He looked touched and amused at the same time as

he pulled the sleigh to a stop in front of the lodge. "I've been warned, I guess."

"You have," she said firmly. "Addie is lucky to have you for a father. Any child would be."

His expression warmed and he gazed down at her long enough that she started wondering if he might kiss her again. Instead, he climbed down from the sleigh, then held a hand up to help her out.

She hesitated, thinking she would probably be wise to make her way down by herself on the complete opposite side of the sleigh from him. But for the last ten minutes, they had been interacting with none of the recent awkwardness and she didn't want to destroy this fragile peace.

She took his hand and stepped gingerly over the side of the sleigh.

"Careful. It's icy right there," he said.

The words were no sooner out of his mouth when her boot slipped out from under her. She reached for the closest handhold, which just happened to be the shearling coat covering the muscled chest of a six-foot-two-inch male. At the same moment, he reacted instinctively, grabbing her close to keep her on her feet.

She froze, aware of his mouth just inches from hers. It would be easy, so easy, to step on tiptoe for more of those delicious kisses.

His gaze locked with hers and she saw a raw hunger there that stirred answering heat inside her.

The moment stretched between them, thick and rich like Aunt Mary's hot cocoa and just as sweet.

Why was she fighting this, again? In this moment,

as desire fluttered through her, she couldn't have given a single reason.

She was in love with him and according to two of her relatives, he might feel the same. It seemed stupid to deny both of them what they ached to find together.

"Chase," she murmured.

He inched closer, his breath warm on her skin. Just before she gathered her muscles to stand on tiptoe and meet him, one of the horses stamped in the cold, sending a cascade of jingles through the air.

Oh. What was she doing? This wasn't the time or the place to indulge herself, when a lodge full of young readers would descend on them at any moment.

With great effort, she stepped away. "Hang out here and I'll go check with Celeste to see when she'll be ready for the kids to go on the sleigh."

He tipped his hat back but not before she saw frustration on his features that completely matched her own.

## Chapter Twelve

"Wow," Chase said as his daughter rushed down the stairs so they could leave for the Saint Nicholas Lodge. "Who is this strange young lady in my house who suddenly looks all grown-up?"

Addie grinned and swirled around in the fancy red-and-gold velvet dress she was wearing to perform her musical selection with Olivia and Louisa. "Thanks, Dad," she said. "I love this dress *so much*! I wish I could keep it but I have to give it back after the show tonight so maybe someone else can wear it for next year's Christmas show."

"Those are the breaks in show business, I guess," he said. "You've got clothes to change into, right?"

She held up a bag.

"Good. Are you're sure you don't need me to braid your hair or something?"

He was awful with hair but had forced himself to learn how to braid, since it was the easiest way to tame Addie's curls.

"No. Faith said she would help me fix it like Louisa and Olivia have theirs. That's why I have to hurry."

"Yes, my lady. Your carriage awaits." He gave an exaggerated bow and held out her coat, which earned him some of Addie's giggles.

"You're so weird," she said, with nothing but affection in her voice.

"That's what I hear. Merry Christmas, by the way."

She beamed. "I'm so glad we're having our pretend Christmas Eve on the same night as the show. It's perfect."

He buttoned up her coat, humbled by the way she always tried to find a silver lining. "Even though we can't spend the whole evening playing games and opening presents, like we usually do?"

"You only let me open one present on Christmas Eve," she reminded him. "We can still do that after the show, and then tomorrow we'll open the rest of them on our fake Christmas morning."

"True enough."

"Presents are fun and everything. I love them. Who doesn't?"

"I can't think of anyone," he replied, amused by her serious expression.

"But that's not what Christmas is really about. Christmas is about making other people happy—and our show will make a lot of lonely older people very happy. That's what Faith said, anyway."

His heart gave a sharp little jolt at her name, as it always did. "Faith is right," he answered.

About the show, anyway. She wasn't right about him, about them, about the fear that was holding her back from giving him a chance. He couldn't share that with his child so he merely smiled and held open the door for her.

"Let's go make some people happy," he said.

Her smile made her look wiser than her eleven years, then she hurried out into the December evening.

Three hours later, he stood and clapped with the delighted audience as the children walked out onto the small stage at the Saint Nicholas Lodge to take their final bow.

"That was amazing, wasn't it?" Next to him, Flynn beamed at his own daughter, Olivia, whose red-and-gold dress was a perfect match to those worn by Louisa and Addie.

"Even better than last year, which I didn't think was possible," Chase said.

"Those kids have truly outdone themselves this year," Flynn said, gazing out at the smiles on all the wrinkled and weathered faces in the audience as they applauded energetically. "Like it or not, I have a feeling this show for the senior citizens of Pine Gulch has now officially entered into the realm of annual traditions."

Chase had to agree. He had suspected as much after seeing the show the previous year. Though far from an elaborate production—the cast only started rehearsing the week before, after all—the performance was sweet and heartfelt, the music and dancing and dramatic performances a perfect mix of traditional and new favorites.

Of course the community would love it. How could they do otherwise?

"I'm a little biased, but our girls were the best," Flynn said.

Again, Chase couldn't disagree. Olivia had a pure, beautiful voice that never failed to give him chills, while Lou and Addie had done a more than adequate job of backing her up on a stirring rendition of "Angels We Have Heard on High" that had brought the audience to its feet.

"I overheard more than one person saying that was the highlight of the show," Chase said.

He knew Flynn had become more used to his daughter onstage over the last year as she came out of her shell a little more after witnessing the tragedy of her mother's death. While Flynn would probably never love it, he appeared to be resigned to the fact that Olivia, like her mother and grandmother before her, loved performing and making people happy.

Almost without conscious intention, his gaze strayed to Faith, who was hugging the children as they came offstage. She wore a silky red blouse that caught the light and she had her hair up again in a soft, romantic style that made him want to pull out every single pin.

She must have felt his attention. She looked up from laughing at something cute little Jolie Wheeler said and her gaze connected with his. Heat instantly sparked between them and he watched her smile slip away and her color rise.

They gazed at each other for a long moment. Neither of them seemed in a hurry to look away.

He missed her.

He hadn't really spoken with her since that sleigh ride the other night. She had seemed to avoid him for the rest of that evening, and he and Addie hadn't made it to Sunday dinner that week.

When he dropped Addie off earlier in the evening, he had greeted Faith, of course, but she had seemed frazzled and distracted as she hurried around helping the children with hair and makeup.

He hadn't had time to linger then anyway, as Rafe had sent him out to pick up some of the senior citizen guests who didn't feel comfortable driving at night amid icy conditions.

Now Jolie asked her a question and Faith was forced to look down to answer the girl, severing the connection between them and leaving him with the hollow ache that had become entirely too familiar over the last few weeks.

More than anything, he wished he knew what was in her head.

Addie came offstage and waved at him with an energy and enthusiasm that made Flynn laugh.

"I think someone is trying to get your attention," his friend said to Chase in a broad understatement.

"You think?" With a smile, Chase headed toward his daughter.

"Did you see me, Dad?" she exclaimed.

"It was my very favorite part of the show," he told her honestly.

"Lots of other people have told us that, too. We *were* good, but everyone else was, too. I'm so glad I got to do it, even though I missed the first rehearsals."

"So am I."

She hugged him and he felt a rush of love for his sweet-natured daughter.

"What now?" he asked.

"I need to change out of the dress and give it back, I guess," she said, her voice forlorn.

"You sound so sad about that," Faith said from behind him.

He hadn't seen her approach and the sound of her voice so near rippled down his spine as if she had kissed the back of his neck.

Addie sighed. "I just love this dress. I wish I could keep it. But I understand. They need to keep it nice for someone else to wear next year."

Faith hugged her. "Sorry, honey. I took a thousand pictures of you three girls, though. You did such a great job."

Addie grinned. "Thanks, Faith. I *love* my hair. Thank you for doing it. I wish it could be like this every day."

"You are so welcome, my dear," she said with a smile that sent a lump rising in his throat. These were the two females he loved most in the world, with Louisa, Mary and Faith's sisters filling in the other slots, and he loved seeing them interact.

"I guess I should be wishing you a Merry Christmas Eve," Faith said.

"It's the best Christmas Eve on December 20 I ever had," Addie said with a grin, which made Faith laugh.

The sound tightened the vise around his chest. She hadn't laughed nearly enough over the last three years.

What would everyone in the Saint Nicholas Lodge do if he suddenly tugged her to him and kissed her firmly on the mouth for all to see?

"What's for Christmas Eve dinner?" Faith asked him before he could think about acting on the impulse.

He managed to wrench his mind away from impossible fantasies. "You know what a genius I am in the kitchen. I bought a couple of takeout dinners from the café in town. We *are* having a big breakfast tomorrow, though. I can handle waffles and bacon."

"Why don't you eat your Christmas Eve dinner here? We have so much food left over. I think Jenna always overestimates the crowd. Once the crowd clears, we're going to pull some of it out. Everyone is starving, since we were all too busy for dinner before the show to take time for food. You're more than welcome to stay— though I completely understand if you have plans at home for your Christmas Eve celebration."

"Can we, Dad?" Addie begged. "I won't see my friends for three weeks after this."

She wouldn't see *him* for that amount of time either— a miserable thought.

He shrugged, already missing her. "We don't have any plans that are set in stone. I think the only other thing we talked about, besides the show, was playing a couple of games."

"And reading the Christmas story," she pointed out.

"Right. We can't forget that," he answered. "I don't mind if we stay, as long as you promise to go straight to bed when we're done. Santa can't come if you're not asleep."

She rolled her eyes but grinned at the same time. At eleven, she was too old for Santa but that didn't stop either of them from carrying on the pretense a little longer.

"I'm going to go change and tell Lou and Livvie that we're having dinner here," she announced.

She hurried away, leaving him alone with Faith—or as alone as they could be in a vast holiday-themed lodge still filled with about twenty other people.

"It really was a wonderful show," he said.

"I can't take any of the credit."

He had to smile, remembering how busy she had been before and during the show. The previous year had been the same. She claimed she wanted nothing to do with the holiday show, then pitched in and did whatever was necessary to pull it off.

His smile slid away when he realized she was gazing at his mouth again.

Yeah. He decided he didn't much care what people would think if he kissed her again right now.

She swallowed and looked away. "I need to, um, probably take Sparkle back to the barn for the night."

Besides the musical number with Addie and her friends, the other highlight of the show had been when

Celeste, under duress, read from her famous story "Sparkle and the Magic Snowball" to the captivated audience while the *real* Sparkle stood next to her, looking for all the world as if he were reading the story over her shoulder.

"I'll help," he offered.

Both of them knew she didn't need his help but after a moment, she shrugged and headed toward the front door and the enclosure where Sparkle hung out when he made appearances at the lodge.

Faith paused long enough to grab her coat off the rack by the door and toss his to him, then the two of them walked outside into the night.

The reindeer wandered over to greet them like old friends, the bells on his harness jingling merrily.

"Hey, Sparkle. How are you, pal?"

The reindeer lipped at his outstretched hand, making Chase wish he'd brought along an apple or something.

"I really don't need your help," Faith said. "He's so easygoing this is a one-person job—if that. I could probably tell him to go to bed and he would wander over to the barn, flip the latch and head straight for his stall. He might even turn off the lights on his way."

He had to smile at the whimsical image. "I'm here. Let's do this so we can eat, too."

With a sigh, she reached to unlatch the gate. Before she could, Ella Baker came out of the lodge, bundled against the cold and carrying an armload of sheet music.

"You're not staying for dinner?" Faith asked after they exchanged greetings.

"I can't. My dad is having a rough time right now so

I need to take off. But thank you again for asking me to do this. I had so much fun. If you do it again next year and I'm still in town, I would love to help out."

"That's terrific!" Faith exclaimed. "I'll let Hope know. I can guarantee she'll be thrilled to hear this. Thank you!"

"I'm so sorry your sister couldn't be here to see it," Ella said. "I hope the live video worked so she could watch it at home."

Hope was still taking it easy, Chase knew, though she'd had no other problems since that frightening day the week before.

"She saw it," Faith assured her. "I talked to her right afterward and she absolutely loved it, just like everyone else did."

"Oh, I'm so glad." Ella smiled, then turned to him. "Chase, it's really good to see you again. I didn't have the chance to tell you this the other night but I had such a great time dancing with you. I'd love to do it again sometime."

It was clearly an invitation and for a moment, he didn't know what to say. Any other single guy in Pine Gulch would probably think he'd just won the lottery. Ella was lovely and seemed very nice. A relationship with her would probably be easy and uncomplicated—unlike certain other women he could mention.

The only trouble was, that particular woman in question had him so wrapped up in knots, he couldn't untangle even a tiny thread of interest in Ella.

"I'm afraid opportunities to dance are few and far

between around here," he said, in what he hoped was a polite but clear message.

"You two could always go to the Renegade," Faith suggested blithely. "They have a live band with dancing just about every Saturday night."

For a moment, he could only stare at her. Seriously? She was pimping him out to take another woman dancing?

"That would be fun," Ella said, obviously taking Faith's suggestion as encouragement. "Maybe we could go after the holidays."

Chase didn't want to hurt her but he was not about to take her up on the invitation to go out dancing while he was standing in front of the woman he loved.

Even if it had been Faith's suggestion in the first place.

"I don't know," he said, in what he hoped was a non-committal but clear voice. "I have my daughter a couple weekends a month and it's tough for me to get away."

Understanding flashed in her eyes along with a shadow of pained rejection. He hated that he had planted it there—and hated more that Faith had put him in the position in the first place.

"No problem," she said, some of the animation leaving her features. "Let me know if you have a free night. I've got to run. Good night. And Merry Christmas in advance."

She gave a smile that was only a degree or two shy of genuine and headed out into the parking lot toward her car.

He wasn't sure how, exactly, but Chase managed to

hold on to the slippery, fraying ends of his temper as they led the reindeer the short distance across the snowy landscape to The Christmas Ranch barn.

It coiled through him as they worked together to take off Sparkle's harness and bells, gave him a good brushing, then made sure he had food and water.

He should just let it go, he told himself after they stepped out of the stall and closed the gate.

The evening had been wonderful and he didn't want to ruin it by fighting with her.

He almost had himself convinced of that but somehow as he looked at her, his anger slipped free and the words rolled out anyway.

"Why the hell would you do that?"

## *Chapter Thirteen*

Faith stared at him, stunned by the anger that seemed to seethe around them like storm-tossed sea waves.

"Do...what?"

"You know. You just tried to set me up with Ella Baker again."

Her face flamed even as she shivered at his hard tone. Oh. That.

"All I did was mention that the Renegade has dancing on Saturday nights. I only thought it would be fun for the two of you."

His jaw worked as he continued to stare down at her. "Is that right?"

"Ella is really great," she said. She might as well double down on her own stupidity. "I've seen her with the kids this week and she's amazing—so patient and kind and talented. You heard her sing. Any single guy would have to be crazy not to want to go out with her."

"Really, Faith. *Really?*" The words came at her like a whip snapping through the cold air.

He was furious, she realized. More angry than she had ever seen him. She could see it in every rigid line of his body, from his flexed jaw to his clenched fists.

"After everything that's happened between us these last few weeks, you seriously want to stand there and pretend you think I might have the slightest interest in someone else?"

She let out a breath, ashamed of herself for dragging an innocent—and very nice—woman into this. She didn't even know why she had. The words had just sort of come out. She certainly didn't *want* Chase dating Ella Baker but maybe on some level she was still hanging on to the hope that they could somehow return to the easy friendship of a few weeks ago and forget the rest of this.

"I can't help it if I want you to be happy," she said, her voice low. "You're my dearest friend."

"I don't want to be your friend." He growled an oath that had her blinking. "After everything, can you really not understand that? Fine. You want me to be clear, I'll be clear. I don't want to be your buddy and I don't want to date Ella Baker. She is very nice but I don't have the slightest flicker of interest in her."

"Okay," she whispered. She shouldn't be relieved about that but she couldn't seem to help it.

He gazed down at her, features hard and implacable. "There is only one woman I want in my life and it's you,

Faith. You have to know that. I'm in love with you. It's you. It has *always* been you."

She caught her breath at his words as joy burst through her like someone had switched on a thousand Christmas trees. She wanted to savor it, to simply close her eyes and soak it in.

*I love you, too. So, so much.*

The words crowded in her throat, jostling with each other to get out.

Over the last few weeks, she had come to accept that unalterable truth. She was in love with him and had been for a long time.

Perhaps some little part of her had loved him since that day he drove her into town when she was a frightened girl of fifteen.

What might have happened between them if his father hadn't been dying, if Travis hadn't come back to the Star N and she hadn't been overwhelmed by the sweet, kind safety he offered, the anchor she had so desperately needed?

She didn't know. She only knew that Chase had always been so very important in her world—more than she could ever have imagined after Travis died so suddenly.

The reminder slammed into her and she reached out for the rough planks of Sparkle's enclosure for support.

Travis.

The images of that awful moment when she had found him lying under his overturned ATV—covered in blood, so terribly still—seemed to flash through her mind in a grim, horrible slide show. She hadn't been able to save him, no matter how desperately she had tried as she begged him not to leave her like her father, her mother.

She had barely survived losing Travis. How could she find the strength to let herself be vulnerable to that sort of raw, all-consuming, soul-destroying pain again?

She couldn't. She had been a coward so many years ago as a helpless girl caught up in events beyond her control and she was still a coward.

Faith opened her mouth to speak but the words wouldn't come.

The silence dragged between them. She was afraid to meet his gaze but when she forced herself to do it, she found his eyes murky with sadness and what she thought might be disappointment.

"You don't have to say anything." All the anger seemed to have seeped out of him, leaving his features as bleak as the snow-covered mountains above the tree line. "I get it."

How could he, when *she* didn't understand? She had the chance for indescribable happiness here with the man she loved. Why couldn't she just take that step, find enough strength inside herself to try again?

"It doesn't matter how much time I give you. You've made up your mind not to let yourself see me as anything more than your *dearest friend* and nothing I do can change that."

She wanted to tell him that wasn't true. She saw him for exactly what he was. The strong, decent, wonderful man she loved with all her heart.

Fear held both her heart and her words in a tight, icy grip. "Chase, I—" she managed, but he shook his head.

"Don't," he said. "I pushed you too hard. I thought you might be ready to move forward but I can see now I only complicated things between us and wasted both of our time. It was a mistake and I'm sorry."

"I'm the one who's sorry," she said softly, but he had turned around and headed for the door and she wasn't sure he heard her.

The moment he left, she pressed a hand to her chest and the sharp, cold ache there, as if someone had pierced her skin with an icicle.

She wanted so badly to go after him but told herself maybe it was better this way.

Wasn't it better to lose a friendship than to risk having her heart cut out of her body?

Chase didn't know how he made it through the next few days.

The hardest thing had been walking back inside the Saint Nicholas Lodge and trying to pretend everything was fine, with his emotions a raw, tangled mess.

He was pretty sure he fooled nobody. Celeste and Mary seemed especially watchful and alert as he and Addie dined with the family. As for Faith, she had come in about fifteen minutes after he did with her eyes red and her features subdued. She sat on the exact opposite side of the room from him and picked at her food, her features tight and set.

He was aware of a small, selfish hope that perhaps

she was suffering a tiny portion of the vast pain that seemed to have taken over every thought.

She had left early, ostensibly with the excuse of taking some of the leftovers to Rafe and Hope, though he was fairly certain it was another effort to avoid him.

He did his best to put his pain on the back burner, focusing instead on making his remaining few hours with his daughter until after the New Year memorable for her.

Their premature Christmas Eve went off without a hitch. When they returned home, she changed into her pajamas and they played games and watched a favorite holiday movie, then she opened the one early present he allowed her—a carved ornament he had made from a pretty aspen burl on a downed tree he found in the mountains. In the morning she opened the rest of her presents from him and he fixed her breakfast, then she helped him take care of a few chores.

Too soon, her mother showed up after visiting her parents at the care center where Cindy's mother was still recovering from her stroke.

Chase tried to put on a smile for Cindy, sorry all over again for the mess he had made of his marriage.

He had tried so hard to love her. Those early days had been happy, getting ready for the baby and then their early days with Addie, but their shared love of their daughter hadn't provided strong enough glue to keep them together.

It hadn't been Cindy's fault that his heart hadn't been completely free. Despite his best efforts, she somehow had sensed it all along and he regretted that now.

He understood why disappointment and hurt turned her bitter and cold toward him and he resolved to do his best to be kinder.

Addie had decided to leave some of the gifts he had given her at the ranch so she could enjoy them during her time with him there, but she still had several she wanted to take home. After he loaded them into her mom's SUV, he hugged his daughter and kissed the top of her head. "Have a fun cruise, Addie-bug, and at Disney World. I want to hear every detail when you get back."

"Okay," she said, her arms tight around his neck. "You won't be by yourself on Christmas, will you, Dad? You'll go open presents at the Star N with Louisa and Barrett, right?"

His heart seemed to give a sharp little spasm. That's what he had done for several years, even before Travis died, but that was looking unlikely this year.

"I'm not sure," he lied. "I'll be fine, whatever I do. Merry Christmas, kiddo."

As they drove away, he caught sight of the lights of the Star N and The Christmas Ranch below the Brannon Ridge.

How was he going to make it through the remainder of his life without her—and without Lou and Barrett and the rest of her family he loved so much?

He didn't have the first idea.

"Why isn't Chase coming for dinner tonight?" Louisa asked as she and Barrett decorated Christmas cookie angels on the kitchen island.

"Yeah. He always comes over on Christmas Eve," Barrett said.

"And on Christmas morning when we open presents," Louisa added.

Faith had no idea how to answer her children. It made her chest ache all over again, just thinking about it.

That morning she had gathered her nerve and called to invite him for dinner and to make arrangements for transferring Louisa's Christmas present from Brannon Ridge to the Star N. She had been so anxious about talking to him again after four days of deafening silence, but the call went straight to voice mail.

He was avoiding her.

That was fairly obvious, especially when he texted just moments later declining her invitation but telling her that he already had a plan to take care of the other matter and she didn't need to worry about it.

The terse note after days of no contact hurt more than she could have imagined, even though she knew it was her own fault. She wanted so much to jump in her truck and drive to his ranch, to tell him she was sorry for all the pain she had put them both through.

"I guess he must have made other plans this year," she said now in answer to her daughter.

Mary made a harrumphing sort of noise from her side of the island but said nothing else in front of the children, much to Faith's relief.

Though her aunt didn't know what had transpired between Faith and Chase, Mary knew *something* had. She blamed Faith for it and had made no secret that she wasn't happy about it.

"Addie texted me a while ago. She's worried he'll be all by himself for the holidays," Louisa said. Her daughter made it sound like that was the worst possible fate anyone could endure and the guilty knot under Faith's rib cage seemed to expand.

Her children loved Chase—and vice versa. She hated being the cause of a rift between them.

"We should take him some of our cookies," Barrett suggested.

"That's a great idea," Mary said, with a pointed look at her. "Faith, why don't you take him some cookies? You could be there and back before everybody shows up for dinner."

He didn't want cookies from her. He didn't want *anything*—except the one thing she wasn't sure she had the strength to give.

"Maybe we can all take them over later," she said.

The three looked as if they wanted to argue but she made an impromptu excuse, desperate to escape the guilt and uncertainty. "I need to go. I've got a few things I need to do out in the barn before tonight."

"Now?" Mary asked doubtfully.

"If I finish the chores now, I won't have to go out to take care of them in the middle of our Christmas Eve party with Hope and Celeste," she said.

It was a flimsy excuse but not unreasonable. She did have chores—and she had plans to hang a big red ribbon she had already hidden away in the barn across the stall where she planned to put Lou's new horse. She could do that now, since Louisa had no reason to go out to the barn between now and Christmas morning.

She grabbed her coat and hurried out before any of them could argue with her.

Outside, a cold wind blew down off Brannon Ridge and she shivered at the same time she yawned.

She hadn't been sleeping much the last few weeks, which was probably why her head ached and her eyes felt as if they were coated with gritty sandpaper.

Maybe she could just go to bed and wake up when Christmas was over.

She sighed. However tempting, that was completely impossible. She had hours to go before she could sleep. It was not yet sunset on Christmas Eve—she still had to make it through dinner with her sisters and their families. Both of them were coming, since Hope had been cleared to return to her normal activities.

They would want to know where Chase was and she didn't know how to answer them.

Not only that but her kids would likely be awake for hours yet, jacked up on excitement and anticipation—not to mention copious amounts of sugar from the treats they had been making and sampling all day.

She should take sugar cookies to Chase. He loved them and probably hadn't made any for himself.

How could she possibly face him after their last encounter?

Tears burned behind her eyes. She wanted to tell herself it was from the wind and the lack of sleep but she knew better. This was the season of hope, joy, yet she felt as if all the color and light had been sucked away, leaving only uniform, lifeless gray.

She was in love with him and she didn't know what to do about it.

The worst part was knowing that even if she could find the strength and courage to admit she loved him, she was afraid it was too late.

He had looked so bleak the last time she saw him, so distant. Remembering the finality in that scene, the tears she had been fighting for days slipped past her defenses.

She looked out at the beautiful landscape—the snow-covered mountains and the orange and yellows of the sunset—and gave in to the torment of her emotions here, where no one could see her.

After a few moments, she forced herself to stop, wiping at the tears with her leather gloves. None of this maudlin stuff was helping her take care of her chores and now she would have to finish quickly so she could hurry back to the house to fix her makeup before her sisters saw evidence of her tears and pressed her about what was wrong.

How could she tell them what a mess she had made of things?

With another sigh, she forced herself to focus on the job at hand. She walked through the snow to the barn and pushed the door open but only made it a few steps before she faltered, her gaze searching the interior.

Something was wrong.

Over the past two and a half years, she had come to know the inside of this barn as well as she did her own bedroom. She knew it in all seasons, all weather, all moods.

She knew the scents and the sounds and the shift-ing light—and right now she could tell something was different.

Someone was here.

She moved quietly into the barn, reaching for the pitchfork that was usually there. It was missing but she found a shovel instead and decided that would have to do.

No one else should be here.

She had two part-time ranch hands but neither was scheduled to be here on Christmas Eve. She had given both time off for the holidays and didn't expect to see them until the twenty-seventh. Anyway, if it had been Bill or Jose, wouldn't she have seen their vehicles parked out front?

With the shovel in hand, she headed farther into the interior of the big barn, eyes scanning the dim interior. Seconds later she spotted it—a beautiful paint mare in one of the stalls near the far end of the barn.

At almost that exact moment, she heard a noise com-ing from above her. She whirled toward the hayloft that took up one half of the barn and spotted him there, his back to her, along with the missing pitchfork.

"Chase!" she exclaimed. "What are you doing here?"

He swiveled around, and for an arrested moment, he looked at her with so much love and longing, she almost wept again.

Too quickly, he veiled his features. "Feeding Lou's new horse. While I was at it, I figured I could take care of the rest of your stock in the barn so you wouldn't have to worry about it tonight. I was hoping to get out of here before you came down from the house but obviously I'm not fast enough."

He had done that for her, even though he was furious with her. She wanted to cry all over again.

Happiness seemed to bloom through her like springtime and the old barn had never looked so beautiful.

She swallowed, focusing on the least important thought running through her head. "How did you get the new horse down here? I never saw your trailer."

"I didn't want Lou to see it and wonder what was going on so I came in the back way, down the hill. I rode Tor and tied the mare's lead line to his saddle."

"You came down through all that snow?" she exclaimed. "How on earth did you manage that?" There were drifts at least four feet deep in places on that ridgeline.

"It was slow going but Tor is tough and so's the new little mare. She's going to be a great horse for Lou."

She felt completely overwhelmed suddenly, humbled and astonished that he would go to such lengths for her daughter.

And for her, she realized.

This was only one of a million other acts over the last few years that provided all the evidence anyone could need that he loved her.

"I can't believe you would do that."

"Don't make a big deal out of it," he said, his tone distant.

"It is a big deal to me. It's huge. Oh, Chase."

The tears from earlier broke free again and a small

sob escaped before she could cover her mouth with her fingers.

"Cut it out. Right now."

She almost laughed at the alarm in his voice, despite the tears that continued to trickle down her cheeks.

"I can't. I'm sorry. When the man I love shows me all over again how wonderful he is, I tend to get emotional. You're just going to have to deal with that."

Her words seemed to hang in the air of the barn like dust motes floating in the last pale shafts of Christmas Eve sunlight. He stared at her for a second, then lurched toward the ladder. Before he reached it, his boot heel caught on something. He staggered for just a moment and tried to regain his balance but he didn't have anything to hold on to.

He fell in what felt like slow motion, landing with a hard thud that sounded almost as loud as her instinctive scream.

He couldn't breathe—and not because her words had stunned him. No. He literally couldn't breathe.

For a good five seconds, his lungs were frozen, the wind knocked hard out of him. He was aware on some level of her running toward him to kneel next to him, of her panicked, tearstained features and her hands on his face and her cries of "breathe, breathe, *breathe*."

He wasn't sure if the advice was for him or herself but then, just as abruptly, the spasm in his diaphragm eased and he could inhale again, a small breath and then increasingly deeper until he dared talk again.

"I'm...okay."

She was reaching for her phone when he spoke. At his voice, she gasped, dropping it to the concrete floor of the barn and throwing herself across him with an impact that made him grunt.

She immediately eased away. "Where does it hurt? I need to call an ambulance. It will probably take them a while to get here so it might be faster for me to just drive you."

The panic in her voice seeped through his discomfort and he reached out a hand to cover hers.

"I don't...need an ambulance. The breath...was knocked out of me...but I'm okay."

The alfalfa he had been forking down for the animals had cushioned most of the impact and he knew there was no serious damage, even though everything still ached. He might have a broken rib in there, but he wasn't about to tell her that.

"Are you sure? That was a hard fall."

"I'm sure."

Her hand fluttered in his and he suddenly remembered what she had said and his complete shock that had made him lose his footing.

He sat up and wiped at her tears.

"Faith. What were you saying just before I fell?"

She looked down, her cheeks turning pink. "I... Nothing."

It was the exact antithesis of *nothing*. "You said you loved me," he murmured.

She rubbed her cheek on her shoulder as if trying to hide evidence of the tears trickling down. "That was a pretty hard fall," she said again. "Are you sure you didn't bump your head, too?"

"Positive. I know what I heard. Why do you think I fell? You shocked me so much I forgot I was ten feet up in the air. Say it again."

Her hand fluttered in his again but he held it tight. He wasn't going to let her wriggle away this time. After a moment, she stopped and everything about her seemed to sigh.

"I love you," she whispered. "I've known it for a while now. I just… I've been so afraid."

"I know. I'm sorry."

He hadn't wanted to make her suffer more than she already had. But maybe they both had to pass through this tough time to know they could make it through to the other side.

He pulled her toward him and his breath seemed to catch all over again—and not at all from the pain—when she wrapped her arms around his waist and rested her cheek against his chest.

Joy began to stir inside him, tentative at first and then stronger.

She belonged exactly here. Surely she had to know that by now.

"After Travis died, I never wanted to fall in love again. Ever," she said, her voice low. "I guess it's a good thing I didn't."

He frowned in confusion, nearly groaning at the possibility of more mixed signals from her.

And then she kissed him. Just like that. She lifted her head, found his mouth and kissed him with a fierce emotion that sent joy rushing through him like the Cold Creek swollen with runoff.

"I didn't need to fall in love," she said, her beautiful eyes bright with more tears and a tenderness that made *him* want to weep. "I was already there, in love with my best friend. That love surrounded me every moment of every day. I just had to find the strength to open my heart to it."

"And have you?"

She kissed him again in answer and he decided he wanted to spend every Christmas Eve right here with her in her barn, surrounded by animals and hay and possibilities.

He had no idea how all his Christmas wishes had come true but he wasn't about to question it.

"I love you, Chase Brannon," she murmured against his mouth.

He didn't want to ask but he had to know. "What changed?"

"Why am I not afraid to admit I love you?" She smiled a little. "Who said I'm not? But I have been thinking about something my dad told us over and over when we were held prisoner in Colombia. *Remember, girls*, he would say in that firm voice. *Faith is always stronger than fear.* He was talking about faith in the abstract, not me in particular, but I have decided to listen to his words and apply them to me. I can't let my fear control me. I *am* stronger than this—and during the times when I'm not, I've got your strength to lean on."

He kissed her, humbled and overwhelmed and incredibly grateful for this amazing woman in his arms,

who had been through incredible pain but came through
with grace, dignity and a beautiful courage.

He wiped a tear away with his thumb, grateful beyond words that such a woman was willing to face her
completely justifiable fears for *him*.

"I thought I was going to have a heart attack just now
when you fell. For an instant, it was like Travis all over
again—but it also confirmed something I had already
been thinking."

"Oh?"

She pressed her cheek against his hand. "I've been
worried that I'm not strong enough to open my heart
to you. The real question is whether I'm strong enough
to live without you. When I saw you fall, in those horrible few seconds when you weren't breathing, I realized the answer to that is an unequivocal, emphatic no.
I can't bear the idea of not being with you."

He couldn't promise nothing would ever happen to
him—but he could promise he would love her fiercely
every single day of his life.

"I love you, Chase. I love you, my kids love you, my
entire family loves you. I need you. You are my oldest
and dearest friend—and my oldest and dearest love."

He framed her face in his hands and kissed her with
all the pent-up need from all these years of standing on
the sidelines, waiting for their moment to be right. He
almost couldn't believe this was real. Maybe he was
simply hallucinating after having the wind knocked
out of him. But his senses seemed even more acute
than usual, alive and invigorated, and the joy expand-

ing in his chest was too bright and wild and beautiful to be imaginary.

People said Christmas was a time for miracles.

He would never doubt that again.

## *Epilogue*

*Christmas Eve, one year later*

"Okay, help me out, Mary. Where do you keep the salad tongs since you and Pat have renovated the kitchen?"

With whitewashed cabinets and new stainless steel appliances, the new Star N kitchen was beautiful, Faith had to admit—almost as pretty as the renovated kitchen at the Brannon Ridge that had been her wedding present from Chase. But after two months, she still couldn't seem to figure out how to find things here now.

Mary headed to a large drawer on the island. "It made more sense to keep all the utensils in the biggest drawer here where they can all fit instead of scattered throughout the kitchen. I don't know why it took me fifty years to figure that out. Is this what you're look-ing for?"

"Yes! Thank you."

She added the dressing to the rest of the ingredients in her favorite walnut cranberry salad and tossed it with the tongs. "There. That should do it. Everything looks great, Mary."

"Thanks." Her aunt beamed and Faith thought, not for the first time, that Mary seemed years younger since her marriage to Pat.

"Thank you for hosting the party here at the Star N."

"Christmas is about home and this old house is home to you girls," Mary said simply. "It seemed right, even though all of you have bigger places now. Your kitchen up at Brannon Ridge is twice the size as this one."

As they were discussing how they would merge their lives after they were married, she and Chase had looked at both houses and decided to run both ranches from Brannon Ridge. The house was bigger for all three of their kids and assorted horses, dogs and barn cats.

It had been a good decision, confirmed just a few months after Faith and Chase's wedding, when Mary announced she and her beau were getting married and wanted to renovate the Star N—a process now in the final phases.

"Anything else I can carry out to the dining room?" she asked.

"I made a fruit salad, too. It's in the refrigerator," Mary said.

Faith grabbed it and, with one bowl under each arm,

headed for the two long tables that had been set up in the great room to hold the growing family.

She was arranging the bowls when Hope wandered over. "Hey, do you have any idea where I can find tape? I've still got one present to wrap."

"Let me get this straight. You run the most famous Christmas attraction in the Intermountain West *and* you've illustrated a holiday book that was turned into a movie currently ranked number one at the box office for the fourth consecutive week. Yet here it is five p.m. on Christmas Eve and you're still not finished wrapping your presents?"

"Oh, give me a break. I've had a little bit on my plate. You would not *believe* how much of my day this little creature takes up."

Faith smiled. "I think I would. I've had two of my own, remember? Here. Give."

Her sister held up the wriggling adorableness that was her six-month-old son, Samuel, born healthy and full-term, with no complications whatsoever from that early scare more than a year ago.

"You can have him if you tell me where I can find tape."

"The desk drawer in the office." She grinned and admitted the truth. "That's where I put it a half hour ago, anyway, when I finished wrapping my last present."

Hope snorted but fulfilled her part of the deal by handing over the boy.

After she left, Faith nuzzled his neck. Oh, he smelled delicious. Her heart seemed to burst with happiness. "Hey, Sammy. How's my favorite guy?"

"Wow. I guess that puts us in our place, right, Barrett?"

She looked up to find Chase and her son in the doorway, stomping snow off their boots after coming in from shoveling the driveway.

He was smiling but she didn't miss the light in his gaze as he watched her cuddle Hope's cute little boy.

How was it possible that, even after a year, she loved Chase more every single time she saw him?

"My favorite *little* guy," she amended. "You two are my favorite bigger guys. How's the snow out there?"

"Still coming down," Chase said. "Mary said she thinks we'll get another six or seven inches out of the storm. Perfect for cuddling in by the fire and hanging out with the family on Christmas morning."

"I hope Celeste and Flynn make it."

"They pulled in right as we were finishing the driveway," he assured her.

"That's good," Mary said from the kitchen. "Everything's ready and I'm *starving*."

"Sorry we're late," Celeste said as she, Flynn and Olivia came in with their arms loaded down with gifts.

"We still had to wrap a couple of presents," Olivia explained.

Hope paused in the act of setting her hastily wrapped final present under the big tree in the window. "Seriously, CeCe? On Christmas Eve? Maybe next year you should plan ahead a little better," she said virtuously.

Faith had to laugh, which ended up startling Sammy. "Sorry, kiddo."

"Here, I'll take him back."

She didn't want to surrender the soft little bundle

but Mary came in just then. "Great. Everybody's here. Find your places."

After handing Sammy back to his mother, she found a place beside Chase. Addie and Louisa sat at her other side while Barrett sat on Chase's other side.

When they were all settled, Celeste looked around at their family.

"I have an announcement to make. *We* do, actually."

Olivia, Faith noticed, was just about jumping out of her chair in excitement.

"Is this about *Sparkle and the Magic Snowball* being number one again at the box office?" Addie asked.

"Everybody knows that already," Olivia said.

"Is it about the new Sparkle book that's coming out next summer or the movie sequel they're already making?" Louisa asked.

"No," Flynn said. "Though that's all very exciting."

He reached for Celeste's hand and Faith held her breath, sensing what was coming next before her sister even said it.

"We're having a baby."

The table erupted into squeals of excitement and hearty congratulations.

"Another baby. What wonderful news—and the perfect time to find out, on Christmas Eve," Mary exclaimed, her features soft with delight. "When are you due?"

"June. Right around the book launch, which isn't the greatest of timing, I know."

"We'll figure it out," Hope said. "This is so great!

Maybe you'll have a boy, too, and he and Sammy can be best friends!"

Faith felt a big, strong hand reach out and grip hers. She glanced at her husband and saw a secret little smile there, the same one exploding in her heart. The two new cousins would soon become three, but she and Chase were the only ones at the table who knew that, for now.

They wouldn't share their news yet. Faith was only eight weeks along and they had decided to wait until after the New Year to tell anyone. Even Barrett, Lou and Addie didn't know yet.

It was tough to keep the news under wraps but there would be time enough to let the family know even more joy would soon be on the way.

For now, she would celebrate her sister's happiness.

Her heart seemed filled to overflowing and tears welled up as she looked around the table at her family, these people she loved so much.

Pregnancy hormones were making her *crazy*. She cried at everything these days. This, the chance to spend Christmas Eve with all the people she loved most in the world, was worth a few tears, she decided.

Chase's strong, callused fingers threaded through hers and more tears leaked out. He nudged her shoulder with his, and then her oldest and dearest friend—and the man she loved with all her heart—handed her his napkin so she could dry her tears.

"What's wrong? Why are you crying, Mom?" Louisa asked, concern in her eyes that could look so fierce and determined when she and the horse she adored galloped through a barrel course.

Faith sniffled a little more. "I'm happy. That's all."

"Cut it out or you'll set me off," Celeste said.

"And me," Hope said. "Since I had Sammy, I cry if the wind blows at me from the wrong direction."

Faith gave her sisters a watery smile. Their father's words certainly held true for his daughters. Each of them had proved that faith *was* stronger than fear, that they could move past the tough experiences in their past and let love help them heal.

She tightened her fingers around Chase's, the joy in her heart blazing as brightly as the lights on Aunt Mary's big Christmas tree that sent out warmth and color and hope across the snowy night.

\* \* \* \* \*

*Don't miss the other Nichols sisters' stories
of love and Christmas, part of*
THE COWBOYS OF COLD CREEK *miniseries:*

*A COLD CREEK CHRISTMAS STORY
THE CHRISTMAS RANCH*

*Available now from Harlequin Special Edition!*

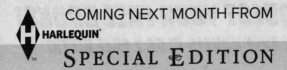

# COMING NEXT MONTH FROM
# HARLEQUIN®
## SPECIAL EDITION

### Available December 20, 2016

**#2521 A FORTUNE IN WAITING**
*The Fortunes of Texas: The Secret Fortunes* • by Michelle Major
Everyone in Austin is charmed by architect Keaton Fortune Whitfield, the sexy
new British Fortune in town—except Francesca Harriman, waitress at Lola May's
and the one woman he wants in his life! Can he win the heart of the beautiful
hometown girl?

**#2522 TWICE A HERO, ALWAYS HER MAN**
*Matchmaking Mamas* • by Marie Ferrarella
When popular news reporter Elliana King interviews Colin Benteen, a local police
detective, she had no idea this was the man who tried to save her late husband's
life—nor did she realize that he would capture her heart.

**#2523 THE COWBOY'S RUNAWAY BRIDE**
*Celebration, TX* • by Nancy Robards Thompson
Lady Chelsea Ashford Alden was forced to flee London after her fiancé
betrayed her, and now seeks refuge with her best friend in Celebration. When
Ethan Campbell catches her climbing in through a window, he doesn't realize the
only thing Chelsea will be stealing is his heart...

**#2524 THE MAKEOVER PRESCRIPTION**
*Sugar Falls, Idaho* • by Christy Jeffries
Baseball legend Kane Chatterson has tried hard to fly under the radar since
his epic scandal—until a beautiful society doctor named Julia Fitzgerald comes
along and throws him a curveball! She may be a genius, but men were never her
strong suit. Who better than the former MVP of the dating scene to help her out?

**#2525 WINNING THE NANNY'S HEART**
*The Barlow Brothers* • by Shirley Jump
When desperate widower Sam Millwright hires Katie Williams to be his nanny, he
finds a way back to his kids—and a second chance at love.

**#2526 HIS BALLERINA BRIDE**
*Drake Diamonds* • by Teri Wilson
Former ballerina and current jewelry designer Ophelia Rose has caught the eye
of the new CEO of Drake Diamonds, Artem Drake, but she has more secrets than
the average woman. A kitten, the ballet and *lots* of diamonds might just help
these two lonely souls come together in glitzy, snowy New York City.

---

**YOU CAN FIND MORE INFORMATION ON UPCOMING HARLEQUIN® TITLES,
FREE EXCERPTS AND MORE AT WWW.HARLEQUIN.COM.**

# REQUEST YOUR FREE BOOKS!

## 2 FREE NOVELS PLUS 2 FREE GIFTS!

**H** HARLEQUIN®

# SPECIAL EDITION

## Life, Love & Family

**YES!** Please send me 2 FREE Harlequin® Special Edition novels and my 2 FREE gifts (gifts are worth about $10). After receiving them, if I don't wish to receive any more books, I can return the shipping statement marked "cancel." If I don't cancel, I will receive 6 brand-new novels every month and be billed just $4.74 per book in the U.S. or $5.49 per book in Canada. That's a savings of at least 12% off the cover price! It's quite a bargain! Shipping and handling is just 50¢ per book in the U.S. and 75¢ per book in Canada.* I understand that accepting the 2 free books and gifts places me under no obligation to buy anything. I can always return a shipment and cancel at any time. Even if I never buy another book, the two free books and gifts are mine to keep forever.

235/335 HDN GH3Z

Name _____ (PLEASE PRINT)

Address _____ Apt. #

City _____ State/Prov. _____ Zip/Postal Code

Signature (if under 18, a parent or guardian must sign)

### Mail to the **Reader Service:**
### IN U.S.A.: P.O. Box 1867, Buffalo, NY 14240-1867
### IN CANADA: P.O. Box 609, Fort Erie, Ontario L2A 5X3

### Want to try two free books from another line?
### Call 1-800-873-8635 or visit www.ReaderService.com.

* Terms and prices subject to change without notice. Prices do not include applicable taxes. Sales tax applicable in N.Y. Canadian residents will be charged applicable taxes. Offer not valid in Quebec. This offer is limited to one order per household. Not valid for current subscribers to Harlequin Special Edition books. All orders subject to credit approval. Credit or debit balances in a customer's account(s) may be offset by any other outstanding balance owed by or to the customer. Please allow 4 to 6 weeks for delivery. Offer available while quantities last.

**Your Privacy**—The Reader Service is committed to protecting your privacy. Our Privacy Policy is available online at www.ReaderService.com or upon request from the Reader Service.

We make a portion of our mailing list available to reputable third parties that offer products we believe may interest you. If you prefer that we not exchange your name with third parties, or if you wish to clarify or modify your communication preferences, please visit us at www.ReaderService.com/consumerschoice or write to us at Reader Service Preference Service, P.O. Box 9062, Buffalo, NY 14240-9062. Include your complete name and address.

HSE15

"The dog wasn't the silver lining." He tapped one finger on the top of the box. "You and pie are the silver lining. I hope you have time to have a piece with me." He leaned in. "You know it's bad luck to eat pie alone."

She made a sound that was half laugh and half sigh. "That might explain some of the luck I've had in life. I hate to admit the amount of pie I've eaten on my own."

His heart twisted as a pain she couldn't quite hide flared in those caramel eyes. His well-honed protective streak kicked in, but it was also more than that. He wanted to take up the sword and go to battle against whatever dragons had hurt this lovely, vibrant woman.

It was an idiotic notion, both because Francesca had never given him any indication that she needed assistance slaying dragons and because he didn't have the genetic makeup of a hero. Not with Gerald Robinson as his father.

But he couldn't quite make himself walk away from the chance to give her what he could that might once again put a smile on her beautiful face.

"Then it's time for a dose of good luck." He stepped back and pulled out a chair at the small, scuffed conference table in the center of the office. "I can't think of a better way to begin than with a slice of Pick-Me-Up Pecan Pie. Join me?"

Her gaze darted to the door before settling on him. "Yes, thank you," she murmured and dropped into the seat.

Her scent drifted up to him—vanilla and spice, perfect for the type of woman who would bake a pie from scratch. He'd never considered baking to be a particularly sexy activity, but the thought of Francesca wearing an apron in the kitchen as she mixed ingredients for his pie made sparks dance across his skin.

The mental image changed to Francesca wearing nothing but an apron and—

"I have plates," he shouted and she jerked back in the chair.

"That's helpful," she answered quietly, giving him a curious look. "Do you have forks, too?"

"Yes, forks." He turned toward the small bank of cabinets installed in one corner of the trailer. "And napkins," he called over his shoulder. Damn, he sounded like a complete prat.

*Don't miss*
*A FORTUNE IN WAITING by Michelle Major,*
*available January 2017 wherever*
*Harlequin® Special Edition books and ebooks are sold.*

www.Harlequin.com

# READERSERVICE.COM

## Manage your account online!

- Review your order history
- Manage your payments
- Update your address

> ### *We've designed the Reader Service website just for you.*

## Enjoy all the features!

- Discover new series available to you, and read excerpts from any series.
- Respond to mailings and special monthly offers.
- Connect with favorite authors at the blog.
- Browse the Bonus Bucks catalog and online-only exculsives.
- Share your feedback.

**Visit us at:**

# ReaderService.com

# HARLEQUIN®

A *Romance* FOR EVERY MOOD™

# JUST CAN'T GET ENOUGH?

Join our social communities
and talk to us online.

You will have access to the latest
news on upcoming titles and special
promotions, but most importantly,
you can talk to other fans about your
favorite Harlequin reads.

Harlequin.com/Community

Facebook.com/HarlequinBooks

Twitter.com/HarlequinBooks

Pinterest.com/HarlequinBooks

# THE WORLD IS BETTER WITH

## Romance

Harlequin has everything from contemporary, passionate and heartwarming to suspenseful and inspirational stories.

### Whatever your mood, we have a romance just for you!

Connect with us to find your next great read, special offers and more.